The Major laughed good-humoredly. "I misjudged you, to accuse you of a lack of humor. I wonder if my reading of your character on other respects has been equally deficient. Shall we test it?"

"In what manner?"

"Like this," he said, swooping me into his arms.

It felt very strange, having a wiry brush of beard and moustache tickling my face. Other than that, it was rather cozy, being encircled in his warm arms there in the cool night air. After a moment, he released me.

"What is the verdict? Was your reading of me deficient, like so many other things you do?"

"Inconclusive. I hold the beard to blame."

"By all means let us blame the beard, and not the wearer. Good night."

Joan Smith

WILES
of a
STRANGER

FAWCETT COVENTRY • NEW YORK

A Fawcett Coventry Book

Published by Ballantine Books

Copyright © 1982 by Joan Smith

ISBN 0-449-50298-8

Manufactured in the United States of America

First Ballantine Books Edition: July 1982
10 9 8 7 6 5 4 3 2 1

Chapter One

God created two perfect objects in this world: the rose, and the diamond. To the delicate rose; He gave thorns to protect it from man's rough usage. The diamond is imbued with a hardness beyond that of any other element. Perhaps this was an effort on the part of the Almighty to protect it. If so, it was not completely successful. Its hardness has never protected it from loss or theft. There is some peculiar fascination in these two objects, the rose and the diamond. Join them together and you have a thing of unrivaled beauty. It was generally agreed amongst connoisseurs that the rose diamond known as the Jaipur was one of the world's finer objects.

Man had connived with nature to enhance the stone's natural beauty. Its original forty carats had been hewn down to twenty-five to eliminate any imperfections. Its drop-like shape was transformed into the classic pear, used often for pendants. Brushing and polishing were carried out by an unknown artisan to bring forth the fire and brilliance contained within. It is one of life's little ironies that this unparalleled thing should ultimately decorate the neck of the ugliest woman in England, the Dowager Duchess of Devontree.

Being one of the marvels of the gem world, it has of course a long and violent history, to which a new chapter has lately been added. I had some part in that last chapter, which began when my father, known in the trade as Diamond Dutch, received a letter from a Mr. Kirby asking him to go to Glanbury Park, outside of Chelmsford, to assess some pieces of jewelry and unmounted stones, with a view to possible purchase by the writer. As Mr. Kirby thoughtfully enclosed ten pounds, Papa did not question his bona fides further, but sat down immediately and wrote off to Mr. Beaudel, the guardian of the treasures in question, to set up an appointment. Mr. Beaudel was as anxious to do business as my father, and answered by return post, suggesting Friday of the same week, at nine in the morning, if that were convenient. It was not, as it meant driving to Chelmsford the day before and putting up at an inn, but my father was so eager he accepted.

"Come along with me for the drive, Mickey," he invited. I have the misfortune to wear a Dutch name, Mieke, which of course has dwindled into the more easily spoken Mickey. Papa is from Holland. He came to England forty years ago and has never returned home since.

"It is spring—the drive should be pretty," he went on. "There is some interesting Roman stonework in that area, and there is the river. Even better, you will see some Flemish influence in the brick buildings—ornamental brickwork, not the plain, raw stuff we get in London." Any echo of his home was always drawn to my attention.

"I'd be happy to go. Beeton can watch the shop."

To use the word "shop" displeased him. He declined to recognize that he had become a shopkeeper. He called himself, indeed the shop sign called him, a consultant in gems. However, he also bought and sold gems—kept a shop—so was what he most disdained, a shopkeeper.

"Beeton can make any appointments that come up," he modified. "We shall be back within a couple of days. A day there, stay overnight, and go to Glanbury Park in the morning. We shall take a day for some sight-seeing afterwards.

Farther along the Chelmer River, there is pretty countryside. You have never been up that way. It will be a holiday for you."

"You are the one who needs a holiday," I pointed out. It is hard to make a living in the gem trade when you work on your own. Customers are scarce and hard to please.

"We'll hire a private carriage and team," he said wildly, the ten pounds burning a hole in his pocket. "The Stag and Hounds is the place Beaudel suggests we put up at. I seem to recall the name. Your mama and I stayed there once."

"It sounds marvelous."

It turned out not so marvelous as we both anticipated. The sky drizzled a cold curtain of rain the whole way, impeding our view of the countryside and casting a pall over our spirits as well.

"What do you know of Mr. Kirby?" I asked, to while away the time.

"I never heard of the man before. I wonder where he got my name."

"Do you know anything about Beaudel?" I asked next, expecting the same brief answer, and already searching my mind for a fresh and livelier topic.

"Beaudel is the guardian of one of the finest jewel collections in the country," he told me, which shocked me very much. I knew a little something of most of the famous jewel collections, but had never heard of Beaudel.

"Which collection is that?" I asked.

"It hasn't a name actually. It is a newish lot brought back from India by Sir Giles Beaudel, who was a big government man there. Governor of Madras province, I think he was. Gem collecting was his hobby. He couldn't have picked a better spot for it than India. The Himalayan ruby mines, the diamond beds of Godolphus, and the sapphires and emeralds from the foothills of the Himalayas. Wonderful gem country, India," he mused, with that special smile his broad Dutch face wore when he spoke of his true love.

"I am delighted to be getting a look at this lot," he went on. "I had not heard it was up for sale, but perhaps only a few pieces are being sold off. I wonder how Kirby got word of it. It is not discussed amongst the merchants in the city.

7

If the really fine pieces are up for grabs, it is such gentlemen as the Prince of Wales and the Duke of Devonshire who would be bidding, and of course such commercial establishments as Love and Wirgmans."

The aforementioned commercial establishment brought a scowl to Papa's face. When he first came to England, he labored in their back rooms as a polisher of gems, a repairer of jewelry with loose prongs or claws, and performed such inferior chores for a very inferior wage. He managed to have a fight with the proprietor in short order. He usually fights with everyone he has anything to do with, except me. Many a deal has fallen through due to his temper. He thinks I am still a child who must be tolerated. Sometimes now he realizes I am no longer young, and then he feels guilty for not having found me a husband, so he is kind to me from pity.

"Is the collection mostly diamonds?" I asked, naming his favorite love. He tolerates the upstart ruby, emerald and sapphire, but has a special place in his heart for the diamond. His little smile said "diamond," as surely as the green haze outside the carriage window said spring.

"The prize of the collection is said to be a rose diamond. It is called the Jaipur. Jaipur is the Pink City, you know. Pink is considered lucky in India. Jaipur is built largely of pink sandstone, and so the pink diamond is called the Jaipur. I have not had an opportunity to see many pink diamonds in my life. It was thought Catherine of Russia had a red one in her crown, but when it was removed for cleaning, it was seen to be an inferior white stone, with a red foil backing stuck in behind it. Kirby asked me to have a look at the Jaipur in particular. Strange I have never heard of Kirby, if he is rich enough to buy it."

"Maybe he is one of the *nouveau riche*," I suggested, envisioning a red-faced beer merchant, wanting a pink diamond for his wife.

"He is putting up at the Clarendon, so he is certainly not a poor man. He could be a nabob," Papa said pensively. "An Indian merchant home from the east with his pockets jingling, and wanting to buy respectability."

He could not set about buying it in a better fashion, in my father's view. Any man who coveted diamonds could not be all bad, or totally common. If Kirby were indeed a nabob, he would be a good potential customer for us, and we were in need of such articles. We were not exactly poor. We did not have to live over our shop, but hired a decent set of rooms in Upper Grosvenor Square, where our neighbors were all genteel. The worry was to set aside something for the future, now that Papa was growing old.

Money had been spared to educate me as a lady, in Miss Phillips' academy in London, as a day student. Our fortunes were to have been made by my older brother, Richard, who was an officer in the Army. We saved up to buy him his commission, but he was killed very soon after reaching the Peninsula. So we rubbed along as best we could, Papa keeping a shop and calling himself a consultant, and I keeping house and calling myself a lady. My father had his Beeton to stand behind the counter, and our home boasted one general female servant of all work.

"If Kirby is from India, that could be where he heard of Beaudel. You said his collection came from there, did you not, Papa?"

"Aye, so I did. That could be the answer. This Charles Beaudel I go to see is not the actual owner. He is only the guardian. The collection actually belongs to his nephew, a young fellow six or seven years old, the son of Sir Giles Beaudel. I daresay the guardian could sell some of it if he thought it for the best."

"It is all a waste of time if the man is not in a position to sell."

"I do not consider it a waste of time to have a chance to see the Jaipur. I would pay for the privilege. Kirby wants me to look over all the pieces, and advise him which are the best buys. A pity you cannot come with me to Glanbury Park, Mickey, but it is a business meeting. If the chap is a good, friendly sort, I shall hint you are interested, and he might invite you to have a look."

"I would love to see the Jaipur. What would it be worth, in guineas?"

"I would have to examine it before saying. If it is without flaw, as rumor describes it, it would be worth a king's ransom, whatever Beaudel cares to ask. I daresay our Prince would
9

hold the populace to ransom for fifty or a hundred thousand pounds for it. By the time the Czar of Russia and King Louis got their bids in, the price might run to any absurd figure you can name."

"It is odd we have not heard of Kirby, if he is in that league."

"Fifty thousand is actually the top sum he mentioned. He hopes to snap it up before it becomes popularly known it is for sale. He seems a shrewd enough customer."

"He cannot know much about diamonds or he would have come to examine it himself. Kirby could be an alias," I mentioned.

"Aye, or he could be acting as agent for someone who wishes to remain anonymous. That is more likely," he said, then lapsed into a reverie while the carriage jostled along the road.

Everyone is fatigued after a journey, even a short journey. We had dinner in my room, after which my father went belowstairs to the tavern for conversation and a few ales. That strain of the Dutch lingers in him, the love of conviviality and the love of ale. I knew before leaving home how it would be, and had come prepared with a guide book to keep me company.

My father was excited in the morning, babbling like a young girl over breakfast. I was happy to see him so cheerful. I assured him I would entertain myself by a walking tour of the town. The parish church was a must, the old bridge that fords the joining of the two rivers another. My book told me the town had been a stopping place on the route from London to the East Anglian ports in Roman days. I also looked for Roman roads and ruins, with indifferent success.

I didn't expect Papa home for lunch, but ate alone at the inn, braving the dining room on this occasion, as the establishment was a respectable one, catering to families. It was not a grand room at all, but the air was redolent of cooking bread and meat, to whet the appetite. The heavy sideboard was set with pewter plates and cruets, the chairs large and comfortable, covered in black leather. An hour passed pleasantly enough.

We had learned that Glanbury Park was five miles away.

As Papa was not back for lunch, I did not look for him for another hour. He had lunched there, obviously. I toured the nearby shops, then returned to the lobby, planning to sit with the farmers' wives and await him. By three, he was back.

"How did the visit go?" I asked eagerly, hoping he had controlled his temper, and returned with a commission in his pocket.

"We'll discuss it abovestairs, Mickey," he answered, with a repressive lowering of the brows that showed he was displeased. *No sale,* I said to myself.

"You disliked the stone? Was there something wrong with the Jaipur?" I asked, my voice low till we reached our rooms.

"I didn't see it. Beaudel says it is kept in a vault somewhere—he was not advertising its whereabouts. What I examined, after a very long wait, was a few baubles not worth the trip. Not a diamond larger than five carats in the lot, and those that were larger than one carat were full of flaws. That is all he has for sale. I got a glimpse, no more, of the better pieces. Beaudel was so cautious he would not even let me pick up one rather fine star sapphire to carry it to the light of the window. An unmounted stone it was. The entire trip was a waste of time. I shall tell Mr. Kirby there is nothing he would be interested in."

"You came all this way for nothing. What a shame!" I sympathized.

"I am disappointed. I don't see why I could not have been allowed a look at that star sapphire. Sixteen rays it is said to have. I do not care for the way I was treated, as though I meant to slip it into my pocket. There was something fishy there. I can't put my finger on it, but I disliked the atmosphere. *He* would select the stones I was to look at, holding the case tight against his chest. His wife had a sly air about her too."

"Mr. Beaudel had never heard of you, Papa. In London circles, you are known. You were a stranger to him, and an unmounted stone would be an easy enough thing to pocket after all. He is nervous looking after someone else's collection. That's what it is," I said, trying to smooth his ruffled feathers.

"He was certainly unhelpful, giving the impression I was not to be trusted. The butler came to speak to him, while I

11

was looking at the better stones, and he called his wife in to 'keep me company,' as he called it. That is when I saw her. To keep me from sliding one of his jewels into my pocket was what the fellow meant. Commoner."

"It is over now. Relax and forget it. Now we can begin our little holiday. The weather is fine today. I have already had a look at the church, but we could..."

"Let us go home," he said, pulling out his turnip watch to check the time. "It is not late. We could be home tonight."

I had seen about enough of Chelmsford to satisfy me. I did not in the least mind departing. "I'll go and pack my bag."

"Yes, let us get out of here," he said impatiently, almost angrily. I wondered if he had come to cuffs with Beaudel. It was entirely likely he had taken offence at his treatment and told the man off. That would account for his mood. Or perhaps he was only feeling he should, by rights, return some part of Mr. Kirby's advance, and was worried about spending more than he had to.

Just as I turned to go next door to my own room, adjoining my father's, there was a peremptory knocking on the door. "Yes, who is it?" my father asked.

"Constable Harper. I'd like to see you, sir," a voice bellowed back.

I stared at Papa, startled. "What on earth...?"

"Get into your own room. Close the door," he said urgently. "This may be trouble. If it is, I don't want you in it. If they take me, you go home. Go to Kirby. Tell him. He'll handle it."

"Papa! What trouble? What do you mean?"

The knocking and hollering were repeated. "Go!" he said, pushing me into my own room, just as the constable opened the other door and barged in. I stood frozen in shock on the far side of the door, listening, but not understanding anything.

"I'm afraid I have to arrest you, sir," the voice said. I put my hand on the knob to pull it open and confront him, but before I did so, my father replied.

"On what charge, my good man?"

"Suspicion of robbery, Mr. van Deusen. You'll have to come with me."

"This is absurd! Who sent you after me?"

"Mr. Beaudel. He reported some diamonds stolen after your visit to him. You are the only one who was there."

"Take a look about my room. You'll find nothing."

"I'll just check your pockets," the constable answered. I could see nothing through the keyhole, but heard some sounds of movement. "Aha! Here we are!" were the next shocking words spoken by the constable.

"What! Where did those . . . ?" A confused, incredulous jumble of exclamations came from my father's mouth.

"Where are the rest of them, eh?" the constable demanded, his tone becoming harsher now. "You pocketed more than five. Eleven are missing from the Park."

I felt the hair on my scalp creep as I stood there, mute, on the other side of the door. How could this impossible thing be happening? My father, Josef van Deusen, the most honest man in the country, was being accused of theft. Worse, evidence of it was found on him. Again my hand went to the doorknob. My instinct was to rush out and tell the constable he was mistaken. There *had* to be some dreadful mistake. My father was suddenly uttering my thoughts aloud.

"There is some mistake," he was saying, and other protests of a similar nature, while the constable insisted he had hidden some stones, and rummaged about the room, opening drawers, looking for them.

"You'll talk freely enough when we get you locked inside a cell. We'll strip you bare, and ransack this room from top to bottom, so you might as well hand them over."

I felt ill, sick to my stomach with apprehension. I didn't know what to do to help him. But I knew what my father had told me to do. Stay out of it. Go to Kirby, and tell him. It almost seemed Papa had expected something of this sort to happen. Why else had he pushed me into my own room and closed the door? Yes, if he were in trouble, and he certainly was, I would be more help to him outside the jail than in the cell beside him.

After some more charges from the constable and protestations from my father, it was settled the bill at the inn would be paid on the way out.

"I'll have to arrange for the return of the hired carriage

13

to London," Papa said, his voice loud. I took the notion he spoke this for my benefit. I was to return to London in the carriage, to see Mr. Kirby.

"Are you alone?" the constable asked, just before they left.

"Do you see anyone with me?" Papa asked, in an ironic vein, for even in this he could not bring himself to speak a lie, so incurably honest was he.

"Beaudel didn't mention anyone else," the constable said, and contented himself with that bit of confirmation. There was a strained cessation of speech while I heard the suitcase being pulled from the top of the clothespress, the rattle of a hanger as the coat was removed to put in it. After a few minutes the constable said, "We haven't got all day. Hurry up."

"I am ready. Naturally I'll want a solicitor to represent me."

"You can arrange that from the jail."

Then the door was opened, they left, and closed it after them.

Immediately, I nipped into his room to look for—I hardly knew what. A message, a clue, a something to tell me what in the world was going on. I found a handkerchief bearing a well-embroidered (by me) *D* in the corner, and beneath it, carefully concealed for me, a portion of Mr. Kirby's letter. It was the bottom half, with his address. The top part of the message had been torn off. "In case of any trouble, I can be reached at the Clarendon Hotel. Leave a message." It was signed J. V. Kirby. I read it twice. What trouble could be expected to arise in the simple examination of some jewelry and stones? My father had made hundreds of such examinations during his life, without once running into trouble. Why had it been expected this time? I wished the rest of the letter were there. My father had expected some trouble, which hinted he knew more than he or the bit of letter told me. And if he expected trouble, why had he taken the job? Upon consideration, it seemed ten pounds was excessive for examining the jewels too. Oh, but it was not enough to repay for this day's work!

I hurried back to my room, stuffed the address and the handkerchief into my case, threw my clothing in after them,

14

and went downstairs to catch our carriage, before it left without me. I expected to feel the arm of the law grab me as I went, but no constable was waiting. I got the carriage in plenty of time, and settled in for some hard thinking during the trip to London. It was imperative to be in touch with Mr. Kirby as soon as possible. The trip would take several hours. It would be dark before I reached the metropolis. Then, before we left Chelmsford, my heart nearly broke with grief.

As the carriage swept through the middle of town, I saw my father being led into the jail by the constable. His head was bent. The jail had bars. He did not glance up to see who was in the carriage that bowled past. He looked defeated, and I was never so furious in my life. I was anxious to confront Mr. Kirby, who had brought this disgrace and misfortune down upon our innocent heads. A jewel merchant's reputation is the most precious thing he owns. A single whiff of scandal would ruin us.

Chapter Two

I went directly to the Clarendon Hotel when the carriage arrived in London. Disappointment welled up inside me when the clerk told me Mr. Kirby was out, and he had no idea when he would return. To wait for him alone at a public hotel late at night was impossible, but presumably he would be back to sleep. I left a note, couched in terms of the greatest urgency, telling him my father was in jail in Chelmsford, and desired his immediate help. He knew my home address, but to prevent any possibility of a muddle, I gave it to him again, and requested that he see me before leaving for Chelmsford. My intention was to cadge a ride back with him.

Then I went home to our apartment to wait. I told our housekeeper, Mrs. Farell, all about the situation, and requested her to tell Beeton, in case my father was gone for a few days. Going to bed did not so much as occur to me. I wasn't the least bit tired, in spite of the exertions of the day, and the lateness of the hour. I freshened my toilette, repacked my little bag with fresh linens, and sat at the window, looking down on the street below for the approach of Mr. Kirby's carriage. For the first hour, I waited fairly patiently, but as midnight came and went, I became not only impatient, but worried.

What sort of a man was this Kirby, that he stayed out roistering till past midnight? Had he not got my note? I most particularly asked the clerk to see he got it. Paid him a shilling to do it. The interval between twelve and one seemed to last an eternity. There is nothing like expecting a thing to happen every second to make the hours drag by. The time between one and two went equally slowly. Between two and six, the hours passed more quickly. I slipped into a light, troubled doze, to awaken as the fingers of dawn lightened the sky. My neck had a nagging crick in it, and both my legs and feet were sound asleep. A million needles pricked them when I tried to stand. The street below was still empty. Not so much as a linkboy or milk cart was in evidence.

As the pangs of hunger made themselves felt, I remembered I had missed my dinner the night before. Mrs. Farell was bustling about by that time, and brought me some breakfast. It was seven by the time I finished. In the emergency that prevailed, seven did not seem too early an hour to have Mr. Kirby roused from his bed, no matter at what hour he had gotten into it. By seven-thirty I was back at the Clarendon in a hired cab, my packed bag with me, to be told by a different clerk that Mr. Kirby was not in. He had checked out the night before.

"That's impossible! He was still registered last night when I was here."

"You'd be the young lady who left off a note? He got it, Miss. I gave it to him myself."

"When did he receive it?"

"As soon as he came in."

"Did he leave me no word, no forwarding address, *nothing*?"

"He didn't, Miss, but he said he'd be back in a few days. He got the message, so there's no need to worry your head." He was looking at me so suspiciously by this time that I blushed for what the man was thinking. I believe he thought

17

Kirby was a beau who was trying to give me the slip. I left, as there was nothing more to be gained from him. I went home and cudgeled my brains as to my next step.

I must be an optimist. What else could account for my taking the idea Kirby had immediately dashed off to my father's rescue? I was not only an optimist, but a spendthrift as well. I went to Papa's shop (or consulting office), rifled the strongbox to get the required funds in hand, hired the cheapest rig I could hire, and dashed off posthaste back to Chelmsford. With some little apprehension I would be recognized at the Stag and Hounds, I went to the other fairly decent hostelry in town, the Shipwalk, which is not as absurd a name as you would think on first glance. Ship is a corruption of sheep. The place was perhaps built on or near a former sheep walk. To conceal my identity, I took the name of Miss Stacey.

There was never the least doubt in my mind all along that I did the proper thing. My father was in trouble, and I must be there to help him. But of what possible help was a Miss Stacey, who did not even reveal her relationship to Mr. van Deusen? Yet to reveal who I was would have the effect of throwing me into jail with my father. I would do him no good there. I hired a cheap room, not knowing how long I must stay, but knowing very well how few guineas I had to spare. I picked up the local newspaper from force of habit, as my father always did when he was registered at a hotel, and went to my little cubbyhole to think. The only thing that occurred to me, and it was but a thread of hope, was to discover whether Mr. Kirby had already come to town. He was not at the Shipwalk, they told me, and after sending a boy over to the Stag and Hounds, I soon discovered he was not there either.

Afternoon was drawing to a close by this time. Weary, dispirited, frightened and ravenously hungry, I had my meal sent up to me on a tray. The Shipwalk was not the sort of establishment where an unaccompanied lady dared to expose herself belowstairs with dark coming on. To reward myself for my total failure, I had half a bottle of wine sent up with the meal. With nothing to be done all evening but sit alone in my room, I dawdled over my food, scanning the Chelmsford paper as I did so. It was largely a waste of time. They carried the week's local news, with a few scraps of national doings. Although it was a weekly, it bore that day's date, which led me to search for the story of the diamonds missing from Glanbury Park. There on page two, I saw my father's name staring out at me, for the world to read. "Suspected in the affair is Mr. Josef van Deusen, a gem consultant" (that at least would please him!) "from London, who was at Glanbury Park at the time. Mr. van Deusen is known in London and internationally by the name 'Diamond Dutch'." There was no mention that he had originally been accompanied to Chelmsford by his daughter, Mieke. For small mercies, let us be thankful. But if the constable had slipped up on that detail, it was entirely probable the proprietor of the Stag and Hounds would inform him, after reading this story.

It was a long article, the whole of it of great interest to me. I read it through twice, to acquaint myself with the details of the family at Glanbury Park. The gentleman Papa had visited was a Mr. Charles Beaudel, uncle and guardian of the owner of the place, Sir Algernon Beaudel, who was a student at Cambridge University. The jewelry, however, did not belong to Algernon. It was the inheritance of the younger son, Lucien, six years of age. The father of the two boys was the late Sir Giles Beaudel, former governor of the province of Madras, in India. He and his wife had both died during an outbreak of some plague in India. It was rather a romantic tale. When the plague broke out, the two boys had been put on a ship home, but the governor was already ill at the time, and his wife elected to stay behind and treat him. She too contracted the fever. They were buried together in India.

The boys were left under the guardianship of the governor's brother, Charles Beaudel. The collection of jewels was only mentioned. Sir Giles had been a small collector before his appointment to India. Some medieval and Renaissance pieces from Europe were the beginning of it. The lack of emphasis on the jewelry did not surprise me. Collectors will often shun publicity, fearing to attract the attention of thieves.

There was a paragraph on Lady Beaudel, the governor's wife. She was the daughter of a noble family who traced its roots back to the Plantagenets. Lord Sacheverel was the pres-

19

ent patriarch of the family. He appeared to be an elderly gentleman, with several sons holding high positions in the Foreign Office and the Army. One was in India.

After two readings, I was more familiar with the background, but no farther ahead as to what my next step should be. When the servant came to take away my tray, she glanced at the paper. "I see you're reading about our famous robbery, miss," she said, smiling pleasantly. She was a young, red-cheeked wench, open and friendly.

"A shocking thing," I said, wondering if she might have any information to add to my knowledge.

"It is, but mind it comes as no surprise to us here in town. No more than was to be expected, says I."

"What do you mean?" I asked, my ears stretching.

"Between the bold young hussy old Mr. Beaudel has married and her carrying on with the lads behind his back and the jewels being hardly locked up at all, it's no surprise at all they're gone. What amazes me is that it's a London gent that took them. I made sure she'd make off with them herself. I'll tell you this, miss, I've seen Mrs. Beaudel in public with diamonds on her neck that don't belong to her in the least."

She had packed up the tray and was heading for the door. "Wait! Why don't you sit down a minute and rest, my dear? You look fagged to death."

"My legs are a mite tired," she admitted, but she did not take a seat. She rested one end of the tray on the edge of the dresser and sighed.

"Have the police looked into the possibility of Mrs. Beaudel's having taken the diamonds?" I asked, making it a casual, conversational question.

"She couldn't have done, could she? They found them on the old gent. Diamond Dutch, he's called. Though they *do* say he got rid of some of them before they picked him up. More are missing than he had rattling in his pocket is what I heard said."

I waited with bated breath to hear the police were looking for Diamond Dutch's daughter, his accomplice. Miraculously, no mention was made of it. "That's true," I murmured.

"Still, I think there's a lot more to it than meets the eye.

What about Miss Little, for instance?" she asked, with a sage nod of her head.

"Who is Miss Little?"

"The governess up at the Park."

"What had she to do with it? Her name wasn't in the paper."

"They wouldn't have known when it was written. She didn't disappear till today."

"Disappear? What do you mean?"

"She's gone. Vanished. Left without a word to anyone, and from what I ever heard, she's not the sort would do a thing like that. Very attached she was to the little lad."

"Did you know her?"

"Not personally, but the whole town's buzzing with the story. She's been gone since noon today, miss. There's some as say she was seen talking to a gentleman at the edge of town, got right into the carriage with him, a stranger, this morning. She might have been talked into running off with him, for they say she took her clothes and all that with her from the Park. Then there's others as say she was killed, and her things done away with to cover it up. I haven't heard it said yet she was in on the job with the old gentleman, Diamond Dutch, but it will be said before long. His daughter *did* come to Chelmsford with him, but it seems she left before he got back from the Park, so unless he tossed the diamonds out the window of his carriage to her, she can't have anything to do with it. Then he would have tossed them all while he was about it, wouldn't he?"

"This is the first I've heard of a daughter," I said, turning aside to hide my nervousness.

"It's what Billie McKee from the Stag and Hounds told me, but two lies leave his mouth for every word of truth. They'll be in a fine pickle up at the Park, with the jewels missing, and no one to mind the wee lad."

"They'll have to hire another governess," I said automatically, but even as the words were said, I felt a giddy stirring in my insides. I was suddenly eager to be rid of the servant. I had some serious thinking to do.

"They'll be advertising right away, I fancy. The hussy that runs the house won't want the bother of a kid. He'll cramp

21

her style too much. Well, I'd best be off. Is there anything you need, while I'm here, miss?"

"Nothing, thank you."

I opened the door for her. She smiled over her shoulder and hastened off with her tray. I was too excited to sit down. I paced the short distance from window to door, scheming how I could get Miss Little's job. There was a deal of scheming to be done. They would not hire Diamond Dutch's daughter. Indeed, they would want references from a Miss Stacey, which she would be hard-pressed to produce.

There were a few letters to be written to arrange the matter. My first was to our housekeeper, Mrs. Farell, to inform her I had minded her three children for the past two years, and given her complete satisfaction. She was to confirm this if the Beaudels should enquire. The newspaper account was cut out and enclosed to help explain this bizarre request. Next I wrote a prim and proper note to Mr. Beaudel, for I had taken a great aversion to his wife. The note explained that I was on my way home to my father's place in Norfolk, making him a doctor so that I would sound respectable. I told a sad tale of Mrs. Farell's children having been sent away to school, and my job being terminated. I had learned at the inn of his difficulty, and wished to have the opportunity of discussing the position of governess with him. Lastly, I tried to think of some way of letting my father know what I was doing. To inform him by letter was too dangerous. A prisoner's mail might be read before it was delivered. Sending a verbal message with an inn boy was equally treacherous. I was still pondering this problem when I went to bed.

Chapter Three

Mr. Beaudel must have been extremely eager to hire a new governess. He was at the Shipwalk to interview me before noon the next day, bringing Lucien with him. I had spent a worried morning walking past the jail, looking at the barred windows, hoping for a sight of my father, without any luck. I had no preconceived idea of how Mr. Beaudel would appear. He was a tall, gentle man, in his middle years, his brown hair receding in twin arcs from his forehead. He was rather pale, and obviously worried. He did not look at all the sort to have been interested in such a dasher as his wife. The boy was a surprise. He didn't look like a boy at all. There was some gravity in him that made him seem a miniature old man. He was small for his age, daintily formed, with silken black hair that any maiden would envy for its soft waves. His lashes were long and sooty black, his eyes blue, his face pale, and his expression very serious. He held onto his uncle's hand, but his attention was all for me. His eyes wandered over me in that frank, disconcerting way children have, missing nothing.

Beaudel had no sooner introduced himself than Lucien spoke up. "My governess ran away," he said. He had a clear, deep voice, with some unique sound to it. Not a lisp, but a peculiar way of holding his tongue that approached a lisp. "Maybe we will hire you, if we like you."

"And if Miss Stacey likes us," Beaudel told him, with a tolerant smile to me, to excuse this outspokenness.

The upshot, before many minutes, was that we all three liked each other very much indeed. This may have been egged along by Beaudel's desperate need of a governess and my determination to be the one selected. He did not even jot down Mrs. Farell's address. He was a pretty good judge of character, he said. I held every facial muscle firm at this absurd statement. I told only such lies as were necessary, and regretted the need of telling any. Beaudel was not at all what I expected. I had hoped I might dislike him thoroughly. My job was to prove him either a fool or a scoundrel. If he had not engineered the deception of concealing diamonds in my father's pockets, he had been hoodwinked by someone who had done so. I had already lit on his wife as the culprit, and was extremely curious to meet her.

"Shall I report to Mrs. Beaudel, or to yourself?" I asked him as we jogged along the road to Glanbury Park. He had not once mentioned her.

"Either one. We both hold ourselves responsible for Lucien. She would have come with me this morning to meet you, but she had a headache. She is prone to migraine, my wife. I wish she would see a doctor."

"Aunt Stella says the doctor makes her sick," Lucien informed me, with a wise little laugh. "It is a joke. He should make her well, but he makes her sick. Why aren't you laughing, Miss Stacey?"

"You offend Miss Stacey to say so, Lucien," Beaudel pointed out, which sent me to look for a reason. I soon recalled my new persona.

"My father is a doctor, you must know," I said.

I would have to be wary to remember who I now was, but at least I could stop being wary about being recognized by

24

some employee of the Stag and Hounds. After some innocuous chatter from Lucien, I judged it not too forward to enquire of Beaudel whether anything more had been heard of Miss Little.

"Not a word from her," he said sadly, shaking his head. "I hope no harm has come to her. She is not the sort of woman I would have thought to behave in this manner. She was very conscientious in her duties. I would be afraid she had met with an accident, but for the fact of her closets and bureau being emptied. The police are looking into her disappearance."

"None of your servants saw her go?"

"They say not. Lucien was the last one to see her. She took him into town yesterday morning. Nothing unusual happened there. They went to some shops to buy a few things, then came straight home. Lucien went to the stables for a ride on his pony, and was told to meet Miss Little back in the nursery. When he went, she was not there. We thought nothing of it at first, thought she was in the kitchen, or even out for a little stroll, as the day was fine. But when she was not back after a few hours, the servants went to her room, and that is when we discovered all her things were gone. She had emptied her closets, slipped away, and left us without any notice."

"I wonder if she might have received word from home— might have been too distraught to leave a message," I suggested. There was something in Beaudel that asked for compassion.

"I would like to think so, but it cannot be the case, Miss Stacey. It shows a kind nature in you to think it. No, the post had come long since with no letters for her. Nor was it possible for her to have taken a coach out of town. The hour was not right. She either walked or was picked up in a private carriage. I cannot think she walked, with a large valise. The police—I spoke to them before going to meet you—have been making investigations. No one saw her walking. She would hardly have headed off through the hills alone. Someone met her. It is a great mystery, but I can only assume it was an affair of the heart," he said, with a passing glance off Lucien, as though to say "we know how it is, but will say no more before the boy."

"Miss Little did not have a beau, Uncle," Lucien informed him, very matter-of-factly. "She often lamented the fact."

I looked at him, surprised anew at his ancient ways. To use such a word as "lamented" was not what one expected of a very child, and to be aware of the state of his governess's heart too was precocious. He looked up and caught me regarding him. He smiled, very slyly, I thought. I made a mental note that we would discuss the matter again in privacy. No stone would be unturned in my effort to prove my father innocent.

"Do you have a beau, Miss Stacey?" Lucien asked.

"You are very interested in romance for a young fellow!"

"I will be your beau, if you like," he offered.

"Thank you, but you are a little too old for me," I replied with a damping glance.

"I don't think so. Uncle Charles and Aunt Stella are a May and December match, and they rub along very well," he answered.

Beaudel flushed a little pink. "Chatterbox. Miss Stacey is not interested in our family matters," he chided gently.

"Yes, she is. Servants are always interested in family matters. Miss Little told me so. She was always interested in us."

"Did Miss Little not tell you that children do not contradict their elders?" I asked playfully.

"I can't recall she ever did, but she told me so many things I may have forgotten a few of them."

Glanbury Park lay roughly five miles from the town of Chelmsford. During the last of the trip, we all fell into an uncomfortable silence. We had said all we had to say to each other, and turned our thoughts inwards. It occurred to me then for the first time that what I was about to do was rash, to say the least. Possibly even criminal. To go under false pretenses to a home about which I knew nothing but evil was at least foolhardy. If I should either disappear like Miss Little, or end up in jail like my father, I would have no one to turn to. Who would believe the word of a prisoner's daughter? The mistress of the house was a hussy, and the boy in my charge

26

wore a strange, sly smile. On top of it all, Mr. Kirby had disappeared. He would be taken for a fabrication, an excuse by Papa to get into Glanbury Park and steal their diamonds.

The countryside at least was pleasantly pastoral. The finer country homes appeared to date from the fifteenth to seventeenth centuries. Many of them were timber framed, some with the elaborate parget fronts, fashioned in geometrical designs. We turned in at a set of black iron gates, drove through a small park, past a stand of firs, to my first glimpse of Glanbury. It was an old home, designed and built before Inigo Jones went to Italy and changed English architecture (for the better, in my own view). There was no Palladian symmetry in evidence. Glanbury was a large, rambling, climbing, sprawling, brick monstrosity of a place, the left side two stories higher than the right, and topped off with a tower. There was a foolish ornamental parapet on the roof of the lower half of the house. The doorway was too small, not even a double door, but only an oaken slab. Some Flemish strapwork was in evidence, as was the patterned brickwork of which my father often boasts. Windows were high and plentiful, hinting at a bright interior. The grounds were pretty. The sun striking the ornamental greenery around the building created a charming effect. In a different mood, the oddness of the house itself might have been found interesting, rather than forbidding.

There was no Mrs. Beaudel on hand to greet us. I assumed that her migraine kept her in bed, or provided an excuse to keep her away from her husband in any case. Odd how I had already taken her in dislike, without ever meeting her. Lucien was accorded the honor of showing me to the nursery and to our rooms. He was a thoroughly competent guide. A fully grown servant could not have been more so, and would in all likelihood not have been half as informative.

"This oak stairway we are mounting, Miss Stacey, was built in the sixteenth century from timber taken off the forests of Glanbury Park. The flowers above us are said to have been carved by Grinling Gibbons. There is some more of his work below. Are you interested in architecture?"

"Very much. I see you are too."

"Not really, but our house is one of the places shown in the guide books, and Lady Schaeffer takes people through it every year, to make money for her charity. I followed her on her tour, and heard her tell people about the staircase. I followed her fourteen times."

"How very patient you are!"

"Not really. She is remarkably pretty, and when I walked behind her, I had an excellent view of her ankles."

"Perhaps you would just step up ahead of me, Lucien," I said, biting back a smile at this youthful lecher.

"I have already seen them, Miss Stacey. Very trim, I might add," he said solemnly. "Our quarters are here to the left," he ran on, as we topped the stairway. "Uncle and Aunt's rooms are over there, to the right. Here is your room. I hope you like blue. Miss Little didn't like it. She found the color cold. Do you like it?"

"Very nice," I said, glancing around at a comfortable, though by no means luxurious, chamber, hung in blue cotton, with a patterned rug and uncurtained bed.

"Your trunk will be sent up here. We shall have to send to the inn for your trunk."

"It—it will be arriving at the inn a little later," I said hastily, although of course it would not arrive until I wrote to Mrs. Farell to pack and forward it. "Where is our schoolroom?"

"It is this way."

We went along to the schoolroom, which was a graceless chamber paneled in dark wood, its only beauty a view from the large windows of the park and winding drive below. Through the branches of swaying beeches, the gate and road beyond were visible. There was a large desk, the one lately used by Miss Little. Various books and schoolwork were spread out on it. There was an open reader, face down at a story about a fox, and there was a sheet on which numbers were written for addition. Lucien was a bright child, I concluded, if he was already adding double digits at six years of age, and reading the book of stories here. I had no notion of puffing him off to his own face.

"This is what you were doing when Miss Little left, is it?" I asked.

He confirmed this with an unenthusiastic nod, but had soon hopped off to hang out the window, trying vainly to reach a bird's nest perched on a ledge below, to the consternation of the mother bird and his new governess. I took a closer look at the books, to notice that Miss Little had been correcting the arithmetic. I could not believe she had had any thought of leaving so suddenly, when she was in the middle of all this work. Surely a governess would wind things up more neatly. She would not leave half an exercise unmarked. She would have finished it, or not bothered to begin.

"Do you want to see my room?" Lucien asked, becoming bored with pestering the birds.

"Yes, please."

"It's next to yours."

We went along to it. Lucien was still sleeping in a child's room. There was no hint of the elegance I was sure must be harbored on the other side of the house. There were well-battered chests and night tables, an open-faced row of shelves holding toy soldiers, horses, books, the paraphernalia of boyish childhood. While we were still there, a servant brought up my one valise from the inn.

"I'll leave you alone to unpack, Miss Stacey," Lucien said, having not only the mind but the manners of an adult. "Shall we meet in half an hour? I'll show you the rest of the house and grounds if you like. In that way I shan't have to have any lessons till tomorrow."

"Quite a little dealer, Lucien."

"Yes, I was forever striking bargains with Miss Little."

"What sort of bargains?" I asked, immediately alert.

"Not to tell things on her, if she wouldn't tell on me."

"Lucien, if you know anything about her disappearance——"

"No, I don't know anything about *that*," he assured me solemnly. I didn't believe a word he said. With a stealthy look at me, he began backing quickly away, before I should interrogate him. I let him go, thinking success more likely if I could catch him off guard.

"Where are you going?"

"I'll be waiting for you beneath the beech tree," he said, pointing to the spot through the window. "That was our meeting place, mine and Miss Little's. Shall it be ours too, Miss Stacey?"

"Very well."

My mind was seething with questions as I hastily unpacked my few things and put them away. I meant to go over every inch of Miss Little's room, in case she had left a clue behind as to where she had gone. The clothespress and dresser were empty of her possessions. Clothing and such personal items as toilet articles were all gone, indicating a fairly thorough packing session. Disheartened, I looked around the room for other possible places. I walked aimlessly to the bookcase, thinking the books belonged to the house. I was considerably surprised to see Miss Little's name inscribed in them. There were three rows of books, indicating a fair investment. Surely a governess would not leave behind the tools of her trade. My heart was beating a little faster as I pulled books out at random to see whether they all bore her signature. Her packing had not been as thorough and well planned as I originally thought.

Looking out the window, I saw Lucien patiently sitting on a white wooden bench by the beech tree, waiting for me. He was not alone. There was a very beautiful young lady with him. Without another thought to Miss Little and her books, I dashed out the door to find my way below to the park, and the beech tree, and Mrs. Beaudel.

Chapter Four

What is it that causes that emotional friction between some people, I wonder? Even before Mrs. Beaudel opened her lovely lips, I knew I would not like her, yet it was difficult to find a real fault in her appearance. She was still youngish, not so young as she appeared from a distance, but young enough to be Beaudel's daughter. She was somewhere in the general vicinity of thirty. Her hair was of pale gold, its shade more reminiscent of moonlight than sunlight. It was dressed too elaborately for a country matron, unless she was to attend a ball. Her gown too was more elegant than the occasion called for, without being quite vulgar. It was pale blue in color, of fine muslin, the ostentation consisting in a ruched skirt, showing eyelet embroidery beneath, with bows attached. It hugged the bosoms closely, and drew in tight at the waist in a manner no longer considered the highest kick of fashion in the metropolis. I did not think it was an unawareness of the current trend that accounted for it. Mrs.

Beaudel did not dress for the fashion, or for women. She was outfitted in a style that would appeal to gentlemen.

Her face was heart-shaped, the nose straight, the lips full and sensuous. But it was the eyes that ruled the countenance. They were not a nice color, rather a muddy green-brown, but they were large, almond-shaped eyes, heavily lidded and heavily fringed. They gave an illusion of her being sleepy. When one looked more closely, it was apparent she was very wide awake.

"So this is your new governess," she said, directing her speech to Lucien, then she turned those orbs on me. They were full of suspicion. I could find no other word for it. She looked as though she would like to turn me off without another word. "How fortunate we are, to have found Miss Stacey so quickly. Quite a coincidence, your being in Chelmsford and looking for a position, is it not, Miss Stacey?" The words were all sweetness and light, the tone sheer vinegar.

"Very fortunate for me as well, ma'am," I answered, with a modest curtsey. "I assume you are Mrs. Beaudel?"

She inclined her head half an inch. "What brought you to town, Miss Stacey?" she enquired.

I gave her my story, then explained it again in more detail as she went over it, questioning me at every word, committing to memory Mrs. Farell's address, asking even a third time what the inn's serving girl had said to me. Of course I omitted that portion of the servant's tale having to do with her. I also kept my temper in check, playing the grateful employee, to conciliate her. After about fifteen minutes of this cross-examination, she appeared to accept me, and condescended to explain her rudeness.

"You know of the troubles we have had recently," she said. "Miss Little running off on us, that wretched fellow from London robbing us. One cannot be too careful."

"I have heard of your troubles, ma'am," I answered briefly, stifling my annoyance, my desire to defend my father.

"I must say *you* look harmless enough," was her final insult, which was accompanied by a slightingly brief run of her eyes over my anatomy.

I have been called pretty upon occasion. Also good-natured, bad-natured, shy and bossy. I was never before called harm-

32

less. Compared to Mrs. Beaudel's voluptuous charms, however, I daresay the word was not inappropriate, as she interpreted it. I noticed that she was looking over my shoulder, and could not fail to observe the little smile she put on, as it created a perfectly charming dimple at the corner of her lips. I expected to see Mr. Beaudel joining us, but it was only the butler. "Only" is the wrong word, as I reconsider it. Hers was a butler like no other ever encountered. He belonged in some fashionable lady's pocket, where I soon deduced he spent much of his time, the lady in question being Mrs. Beaudel.

I was *harmless* enough, and Lucien young enough, that they proceeded to enact an unblushing flirtation under our very noses. Beaudel, if he had any backbone, would have shown this man the door long ago. A butler is usually old, having worked his way up from the pantry. This fellow, Wiggins she called him, was no older than herself. He was tall, well formed, dark-haired and eyed, but with an insinuating manner any real lady would recoil from.

"Would Madame care for some refreshment?" he asked, with a bold smile, as he ogled her from her blond curls to her tiny waist, and back up again, with a longish pause at her bosoms.

"What had you in mind, my dear Wiggins?" she asked, with a batting of her heavy lids and long lashes.

"Madame's wish is my command," he replied, bowing.

She drew in a deep breath and held it, straining the seams of her gown to their limit. "Now, let me think," she said, placing one dainty finger just by her dimple, while Wiggins, the bold rogue, continued to ogle her.

"Some lemonade would be nice," Lucien suggested.

"Could I tempt Madame—with some lemonade, that is?" Wiggins inquired.

"Tch, you are shocking Miss Stacey, Wiggins," she chided. Their eyes met in some secret but meaningful look. "She is Lucien's new governess. Charles hired her this morning."

"Fast work," he answered.

This, of course, was not the sort of conversation one expected to hear between a butler and his mistress. "You will appreciate that," she said, then turned to me. "You must

33

beware of our butler, Miss Stacey. He is a fast worker himself."

"He is not very fast with our lemonade," Lucien pointed out.

Before more was said, a messenger galloped up to the house and dismounted. "Who on earth can that be? Wiggins—you'd best go to the door," Mrs. Beaudel said, arising. "Take Lucien to the kitchen, Miss Stacey. Cook will make him some lemonade."

She darted off to the house, a few steps behind Wiggins. She was certainly curious to learn what message was coming to them.

"So that is your Aunt Stella," I said, taking Lucien's hand.

"Yes, she is very pretty, isn't she? I like her a lot, but she likes Wiggins better than me." Wiggins, not Uncle Charles. Out of the mouths of babes!

We went to the kitchen for lemonade. I was also introduced to Cook and the other servants, who regarded me with suspicion, which turned to acceptance as I behaved myself with propriety and friendliness.

I was as curious as Mrs. Beaudel to discover what news the messenger had brought to the door. I did not learn it until that evening. The interval was passed interestingly enough with the promised tour by Lucien. It was a fine old house, but the details are not important, except inasmuch as I learned where the jewelry collection was kept—in a safe in Mr. Beaudel's study. Oh, and I also saw the master bedroom, which was kept very properly waiting for its master, Sir Algernon Beaudel, who used it on his visits from Cambridge, and whom I learned would soon be its regular occupant, as he was finishing his course that year. Charles Beaudel was not the encroaching sort who considered himself anything but a guardian for the two boys. He was not, from what I could see, trying to take over their domain. I was not shown into Charles's room, but had a door pointed out to me as belonging to Aunt Stella with Beaudel's room next it.

One cannot spend long under a roof without ferreting out the family's little secrets. I discovered that evening that Mrs. Beaudel was bored to flinders with her aging spouse. I ate with Lucien abovestairs, but about an hour after dinner, Mrs.

Beaudel came in person to suggest we join her and Charles in the saloon, "to become a little acquainted," as she phrased it. "For it is so tedious here in the country, with few callers."

Both Lucien and I were eager to join them. When we entered the room, I observed that Mr. Beaudel was perusing the latest newspapers. A pipe had been allowed to go out, but its smoke still perfumed the air, reminding me of Papa, who likes his pipe after dinner. *Would he be allowed to have it in jail?* I wondered. It was no cheerful, domestic scene, despite the pipe. What we were looking at was a tired old man taking his ease at the end of a day, while his young wife, dressed to the nines, fidgeted and wanted to go out, or at least to have someone in. No book, no magazine, no embroidery, no knitting or fringing was in evidence. A half-drunk glass of wine was on a table beside her, forgotten.

Mr. Beaudel arose and smiled pleasantly, made a few jokes to Lucien, then returned to his papers with a sigh of relief, while his wife began flirting with Lucien. It is a foolish word to use, but she was only trying to be friendly, I think, and knew no other way to set about it with a male of any age whatsoever. Lucien was a good little flirter too. He began by saying, "I like your new gown, Aunt Stella. I think it is new, is it not?"

It was a green satin, modishly low in front, which looked very well with her pale blond hair and green eyes. "I'm glad *someone* noticed," she replied, with a sharp glance in her husband's direction.

The newspaper rustled, as Beaudel peered guiltily from behind a corner of it. He was listening then, from his hiding place. He had donned a pair of spectacles. In order to see his wife, he had to look up over the top of them. It added a few years to his appearance, that gesture. What on earth had she ever seen in the man? It could only have been a case of cream-pot love on her side. Beaudel's personal financial position was not known to me, but at least he lived in a fine home.

Wiggins came in to see if Madame would care for more wine. There was no teasing, no flirting, with Beaudel in the room. He behaved properly, only losing control of his eyes for a moment as he bent over Stella, filling her glass.

I was curious to turn the conversation to the messenger,

35

or if not that, then to the diamonds. To my intense satisfaction, Lucien blurted out the question for me.

"What did the messenger want, the one who came this afternoon?" he asked his aunt.

"A man is coming to look at your diamonds," she told him.

"Are you selling some of them, Uncle Charles?" he demanded at once, with a very inquisitive face. What a wise little hammer he was, and not yet seven years old.

"You remember we discussed it, Lucien," his uncle replied, setting down the newspaper. "Just some of the lesser pieces, not the Jaipur certainly. It was your father's intention that some of the pieces at least be sold, to provide funds for your education when you grew up. You cannot expect Algernon to carry all the expense of that for you. If you decide to buy an estate later, after you are older, then you can sell your more valuable pieces. On the other hand, if you join the Army or something of that sort, you may want to keep them. An estate is no advantage if a man is not home to look after it."

"I don't see why you don't sell the lot and have done with it," Mrs. Beaudel said peevishly.

"They might evaluate, bring a better price at a later date," he explained.

"Yes, *might* evaluate, but it is *certain* that money invested would pay good interest. Oh, Charles, I *do* wish you would sell them, and be rid of the worry of looking after them. It worries him so," she said aside to me, with an uncharacteristic concern for her spouse.

It was not my place to venture an opinion, or to pose any questions, which did not prevent me from thinking. I judged Beaudel must have sole authority of Lucien's estate, and Algernon's as well.

"Who is coming to look at them?" Lucien asked.

"A military man. His name is Morrison, a Major Morrison," Beaudel answered. His wife patted the satin material of her skirts, and raised her hands to preen her hair, smiling softly to herself, while I wondered how a mere Major could afford to be buying diamonds.

"Do you know him?" Lucien asked.

"Not personally, but he sent a letter of introduction from your grandfather Sacheverel, so his character cannot be in doubt. I shall be more careful who comes here in future, you may be sure. I shan't let another piker like Diamond Dutch get a foot inside the door. I'll not deal with anyone we don't know, or who has not got a character reference."

"Is he a real soldier?" Lucien asked, while I clenched my hands into fists, and managed to keep my tongue silent.

"To be sure he is. He is a Major. He saw action in the Peninsula with Wellington."

I looked up with interest, for nó other reason but that my brother also saw action in the Peninsula. He was killed at the Battle of Vitoria. It was possible Major Morrison might know him. It was on the tip of my tongue to say so, when I recalled I was no longer Mieke van Deusen.

"I doubt he will be wearing a scarlet tunic," Mrs. Beaudel said. "Since Waterloo, many of the officers have sold out and returned to civilian life. This Morrison has an estate somewhere in Devonshire, has he not, Charles?"

"I believe Sacheverel mentioned something of the sort."

"I wish he would wear his tunic and bring his sword," Lucien said wistfully. "He will have some good stories at least. I would like to be a soldier when I grow up."

"If that is the case, we might just hold on to his collection," Beaudel mentioned to his wife, who rolled her eyes ceilingwards before pointing out this was only a child's dreaming.

The newspaper rustled back into place, Beaudel retired from the social circle, and Mrs. Beaudel examined the cuticle of her right thumb with great interest. This done, she said, "Lud, how *boring!* Do you play cards, Miss Stacey?"

"Let us have a hand of loo," Lucien exclaimed with the keenest enthusiasm.

The cards were brought out, and the three of us sat down to a session of cards. Mrs. Beaudel was petulant, and an indifferent player. Lucien was in alt, and the craftiest little fellow with the cardboards that you ever saw. I was observant, paying more heed to any conversation Mrs. Beaudel cared to make than to the game.

After a short while, she threw down her hand of cards, in mid-game, and said, "This is boring. Charles," she turned and called over her shoulder to her husband. "Why don't you show us the jewel collection? Miss Stacey has not seen it. It will

37

be more amusing than this. Would you not like to see the jewels, Miss Stacey? I'm sure you would."

"I would be very interested to see it," I said promptly.

"*Do* let us show her, Uncle," Lucien added his entreaties. With a fond smile at his wife, Charles set aside his newspaper, removed his spectacles, arose and went for the key.

Stella led the way to his study, where we waited for him. He went upstairs to get the key. Mrs. Beaudel, although she must have seen the treasures many times, was excited to see them again. They were kept in a heavy safe that sat on the floor behind Beaudel's desk. It would have taken two burly men to remove it. The jewels were kept in a wooden chest, covered with brown leather. It was about fifteen inches long and nine wide, the same in depth. When it was opened, it was seen to have drawers, lined in dark yellow velvet, five in all, each shallow. The drawers held an assortment of gems, magnificent pieces of varied sorts. The loose diamonds were kept in the top drawer. There were too many to count—about a hundred, I guessed, varying in size from one carat to five. This would be what my father had seen. It would be from this bunch too that he was accused of having pilfered.

I could profess no knowledgeable interest in the stones, but was allowed a good amateur's enthusiasm. "How lovely! They must be very valuable!" I exclaimed.

"If they were perfect stones, they would be worth a great deal. Indeed, you are looking at about five thousand pounds, Miss Stacey," Beaudel told me.

"Is it some of these the man tried to steal?" I asked guilelessly.

"It was. He got away with eleven, but five were recovered. We made sure the other half-dozen would turn up in the toe of his boot, or in a pocket, but they were not found."

"He got rid of them when he heard the constable banging at his door," Mrs. Beaudel surmised.

"His room was searched carefully. They even looked on the ground beneath his window, but they were not found," Beaudel said.

"Maybe he swallowed them," Lucien suggested.

"I wouldn't put it a bit past him," she agreed.

"How did he take them without being seen?" I asked, with idle-seeming interest.

"He was light-fingered. I'll say that for him. I did not hand the tray to him, or leave him alone for a minute," Beaudel told me. "I daresay I glanced away for a second, and that must be when he slid them into his pocket. It is fortunate I counted them after he left. I don't know how I came to do it either, for I had no reason to suspect him."

"Aunt Stella told you to," Lucien reminded him.

"No! I merely asked Charles if he *had* counted them," she pointed out. "It looked to me as if the tray were less full than before. But let us see the *real* jewelry, dear," she said to her husband. It was the first time I had heard her use any term of endearment. "The diamond necklace that belonged to that Italian queen..."

Charles obediently shoved in the top drawer and opened the next, to lift up a glittering necklace of blue-white diamonds, made in an old-fashioned style, rather clumsy, with a great cluster at the front set in such a manner that no individual stone showed to best advantage. Today they would be set differently, the larger stones having more importance in the design.

"May I try on your necklace, Lucien?" Mrs. Beaudel asked archly.

"I would like to see it on you," he agreed at once. "Diamonds look much better on a pretty lady."

Her husband fastened it around her neck, smiling at her excitement. "I wish I could give it to you," he said.

"You can wear it any time you want, Aunt Stella," Lucien assured her.

"That would not be quite the thing, Lucien. People would talk," his uncle explained. I surmised he had learned that fact by experience. People *were* talking—the servant at the inn, for instance.

"The earrings to go with it," Mrs. Beaudel demanded, reaching out her hand to him, and using the tone more usually employed for servants.

Another drawer was opened, and large pendant ear buckles handed to her. She put them on herself, in front of a mirror that was on the far wall. She had a lamp moved to

39

illuminate the image in the mirror, and a very lovely image it was too. Her eyes glowed as strongly as any of the gems. She adored wearing them, to cock her head this way and that, and see the diamond drops jiggle against her white skin. She fingered the necklace, lovingly, while Lucien admired her, both orally and with his eyes. She coveted those jewels, and it was strange she should be prodding Beaudel to sell them. Of course she could not wear them without causing gossip.

I was curious to return to the unmounted stones, to see just what it was my father stood accused of stealing. I don't know what I had in mind—to see they were only paste, or crystals faceted to look like diamonds perhaps. "How do you know these stones are imperfect, Mr. Beaudel?" I asked, playing the amateur. "You said if they had no flaws, they would be worth more. They don't seem to have any flaws."

"They cannot be seen by the naked eye," he told me.

"You use one of those eyeglass things, do you?"

"A loupe," he informed me, nodding his head. "I have one about here somewhere."

"Could I take a peek through it? I have never used one of them," I lied, with a beguiling smile.

He glanced to see his wife was still being entertained by Lucien before rooting through a drawer for his loupe. That action told me he was no real jewel connoisseur. My father's loupe was never more than an arm's length away, usually in his pocket.

I was careful not to display any expertise with the instrument. I let Beaudel show me how to use it. He chattered on with some unnecessary information. "They tell me the north light is best. I daresay you will see nothing by lamplight."

I saw that the stone, roughly three and a half carats, which he handed to me, had been badly cut, and had a flaw so large that it tended to make the stone virtually worthless. "I see a black mark in it, a sort of line," was all I said.

"The larger ones are all flawed, but the diamond would look well in a ring or a brooch for all that. A diamond is always worth something. Here, try this one. The smaller ones are unflawed."

He let me examine three or four, making sure to get the last back in his hands before letting me touch another. As

40

he said, the large ones were flawed, the small ones perfect. It seemed pointless to go on, but I accepted the last one he selected for me.

The word "carat," as it pertains to precious stones, is an indication of weight, not size. A carat indicates two hundred milligrams of weight. The stone he handed me was about the size a one-carat stone should be, but its weight in my hand felt less than half of what I expected. One comes to recognize what a diamond should weigh, when she has been handling them all her life. I inhaled sharply, but he did not appear to notice. With the greatest curiosity, I held the stone under my eye, but it was a mere formality. Even before I did so, I could feel a trace of roughness on the edge where it had been chipped against the real diamonds. A true diamond does not chip. What I had was very likely a zircon, baked in an oven to remove any traces of color. Zircons chip rather easily. The examination was a mere formality.

I mumbled the word "interesting," and asked if I might look at another of the small stones. The others examined were all genuine diamonds. Somehow, one false stone had gotten passed to me. I considered telling Beaudel so, but even a cursory examination of my position showed me this was unwise.

Mrs. Beaudel was removing the necklace and asking to see other pieces. "You know I do not keep the Jaipur here," he told her, with a repressive stare, perhaps because of my presence. He gave no indication where he did keep it, whether in another part of the house or elsewhere, in a bank vault.

"I don't mean the Jaipur. Let me see the star sapphire," she replied.

He reluctantly opened another drawer to show her this expensive trifle, then another to allow her to pin a ruby brooch on her gown. None of these was examined by me, nor was I so much as allowed to touch them, but they had the look of genuine jewels. Soon Beaudel closed up the box, returned it to the safe, and locked it, pocketing the key.

"Let us have a cup of cocoa and go to bed," he suggested.

From the corner of my eye, I saw Mrs. Beaudel's jaw tighten, but she smiled and agreed to it. "Please join us, Miss Stacey, and you too, Lucien."

"Lucien should be in bed," I pointed out, as it was close to nine o'clock. Eight was a likelier hour for a child to be asleep.

"He can sleep in tomorrow. There is nothing to get up for," she added grimly. "Major Morrison does not arrive till afternoon."

This blatant and public admission that the only pleasure the morrow offered her was the arrival of another gentleman caused Mr. Beaudel to smile deprecatingly. I was sorry I had looked at him.

"It is a pity Algernon decided not to join us for the spring holiday," he said to her. "He would liven us up. We have great times when Algernon is here."

This was easy to credit. A young man of twenty-odd years would be of definite interest to Stella, who was not above flirting with a six-year-old child, and her butler.

"My brother is gone to visit Sacheverel for the holiday," Lucien explained to me. "I wish he had taken me with him."

"He is bound to drop in on his way back to Cambridge. It is hardly out of his way at all," Beaudel consoled him.

"He was here for Christmas," Stella reminded them. "It is only right he spend some time with his maternal relatives as well."

It struck me as decidedly odd she would not be more eager for the company of a young gentleman, but she sounded peevish at the very mention of his name. I wondered if she had come to cuffs with him.

"It is hardly the same thing. Glanbury Park is his own home, it belongs to him," Beaudel remarked.

"Yes, he is not reluctant to remind us of it," she answered sharply, confirming my suspicion.

"Well, shall we have that cocoa?" Beaudel said heartily, to smooth over the incident.

Lucien and I drank ours up quickly. The very mention of Algernon Beaudel had put Stella in a pucker, and she was poor company. But before we left, she roused herself to a smile. "Time you were in your bed, rascal," she said, giving Lucien's cheek a pinch. "We don't want this guy's pretty complexion fading from late nights."

He pushed her hand away, disliking the childish treatment. "Good night Aunt Stella, Uncle," he said, with a proper bow, then he reached for my hand, the first childish move I had seen him make. "I hope you have a good night," he added over his shoulder, as he accepted their wishes for a good sleep.

Wiggins was hanging about the hall, trimming the lamp wicks.

"Good night, Miss Stacey," he said, with a bold smile. "The servants are having a cup of tea in the kitchen, if you'd like to join us. We haven't had much chance to become acquainted."

"Thank you, but I am busy right now," I answered, hurrying past. I disliked his bold stare, his flashing black eyes. I also disliked his listening at doorways, for I was convinced those lamps had been trimmed to death.

"I *do* wish Aunt Stella would not pinch my cheeks," Lucien grouched as we mounted the stairs. He was fatigued with his late night.

He got into his nightshirt with no help from me, feeling himself much too old to require any assistance. "Miss Little used to listen to my prayers," he said, coming to my door when he was dressed for bed. "Would you like to, Miss Stacey?"

"Very much," I told him, arising. I sensed what he really wanted was someone to tuck him in, and was happy to oblige. He might put on the airs of an adult, but beneath it he was still a little boy, an orphan at that, who had lately lost the person closest to him.

My true business at Glanbury Park was not lost sight of amidst this outcropping of altruism. "I expect you miss Miss Little," I said, after he had said his prayers, naming her last in his requests for God's blessing on his loved ones.

"Yes, she was very nice. I liked her," he told me, crawling in, and surreptitiously dragging a well-worn stuffed toy under the blanket, so I would not see it.

"How long was she with you?"

"Only half a year. Before that Mrs. Glammis was my nanny, but she left when Uncle Charles got married. Algernon hired her in London, Miss Little I mean."

I wondered if Mrs. Glammis had not rubbed along with the new bride. To question a child was not a thing I would

43

ever do only to satisfy vulgar curiosity, but to save my father, I would do a good deal worse. "I suppose you have known your Aunt Stella for a long time, have you?" I asked.

"No, only since she came here. Uncle Charles met her last autumn at Tunbridge Wells, where he went for his gout. It was very romantic. They fell in love at first sight, and got married inside of two weeks. Aunt Stella told me all about it."

"How nice."

"Yes, I think she is nice. She is very pretty, and she plays with me. Algernon didn't like it. He said Sacheverel didn't like it either, but they didn't make me move away. Algernon said they might. He was angry at Aunt Stella for turning off some of his old servants, you know, who had been with him for ages, since we came back from India. He told her not to turn off anyone else."

"I expect he was sorry to lose the old family butler," I asked leadingly.

"Yes, he was especially angry about Wiggins. I don't know why really. Wiggins tried very hard to be nice to him. I heard Aunt Stella tell him to be."

"Was Aunt Stella nice to Algernon?" I prodded.

"At first she was, but in the end they didn't even speak to each other. She took dinner in her room the last night he was here. I hope Algernon comes to see me. And I hope he doesn't make me go to live with Lord Sacheverel too. I fear that is what they are talking about, why Algernon went to him now. I like it better here. Grandpa Sacheverel is very old."

"It is cozy here," I agreed, smoothing the blankets, and reaching to brush his hair from his forehead, as I watched closely to see if he disapproved of this maternal gesture. He looked suddenly very young and vulnerable, with his big dark eyes peering at me questioningly.

"Miss Little liked it," he said.

"I wonder why she left."

"She didn't say," he told me, lowering those long lashes to hide his eyes, but not before that sly look had crept back into them. I was certain he was hiding something.

44

"Lucien, if you know anything about her disappearance, it would be wrong to hide it. You know something, don't you?"

"I don't know where she is."

"Do you know anything about her going, anything at all?"

"I know nobody harmed her, Miss Stacey, if that is what you are worried about. I knew she was going. She came and said good-bye, and told me not to worry, that's all. She told me not to tell. It was a secret."

"Did she have a fellow? Is that it, she ran off with him?"

"She didn't have a lover. I told you so already."

"You should tell your uncle what you know."

"I can't break my promise. If you tell them, I'll say you made it up, and then you'll have to go away. I'm sorry, but I promised Miss Little."

"Why did you tell me then?" I asked, angry at being bested by a child.

"Because I like you," he said simply. "And I didn't want you to worry that anything bad would happen to you here. Miss Little said . . ." I looked, waiting expectantly. "She didn't say so exactly, but she kind of hinted I could tell *you*."

"Me? She couldn't know *I* would come here."

"The girl who took her place she meant, whoever she should be."

"Oh," I said, disappointed. "Better go to sleep now, Lucien. We'll have to start lessons tomorrow."

"Miss Little used to kiss me good-night," he said, as though it were a matter of the greatest indifference to him whether I did the same.

I kissed his cheek, and he smiled at me sleepily. "Good-night, Miss Stacey," he said, yawning. "What is your name, by the by?"

"What?"

"Your first name. Miss Little's name was Cecile. What is yours?"

"Oh. M-Mary."

"I thought it might be. It says M. D. on your writing case. What is the D for?"

"The case was a present from my aunt. She had a spare. Her name was Mary too. Mary Daniels," I said, with a quickening of my heartbeat. "When did you look at my things?"

45

"While I was in your room with you. You had it on your desk. I wasn't snooping. You sound angry, Miss Stacey. Are you angry?"

"No, of course not."

"I hope Algernon won't take you in dislike. He will soon be coming home to stay, you know. This is his last term at university."

"I see no reason why he should."

"No, because Aunt Stella didn't turn Miss Little off. And even if she *had,* it wouldn't be your fault. Good-night, Miss Stacey."

"Good-night." I left, to dash back to my room and look for other telltale signs that I was an impostor.

I found none, but I put that writing case in a drawer, and covered it with linens, in case anyone should decide to pay me a visit.

Chapter Five

There was a great deal to think about after I closed the door of my blue room and achieved solitude. Accepting Wiggins' offer to go to the kitchen for tea occurred to me, but I had enough information to sort out for one night. Anything to be learned from them must wait until morning. The one zircon amidst the diamonds was my most outstanding discovery. Beaudel did not recognize it for what it was, or he would not have selected it for examination. His brother, Sir Giles, had been an expert, and certainly *he* had not bought it in error. No, someone had put it there, and if that same someone had not removed a genuine one-carat stone at the same time, I would be much surprised. Stella and Wiggins were at the top of my list for suspects. She knew where they were kept, knew as well where the key was kept, very likely. Between the two of them, they would have no trouble tampering with the jewels. If they had pilfered *one,* it was not unlikely they had pilfered more than one. This gave an explanation for the oddity of my father being accused of having stolen eleven stones, when only five were found in his pocket. They had taken that opportunity to conceal their theft. That telltale one zircon must have been left behind by accident. It would be nervous work, opening the safe. Such an oversight could easily occur.

Beaudel struck me as an honest-seeming man, but it was impossible to judge on so slight an acquaintance. He could be bilking the boy more easily than anyone else. He was sole executor and guardian of the jewel collection, so far as I had been able to discover. It was only natural, however, that Algernon, only a few months away from coming home and taking over his inheritance, would take a keen interest. His altercations with Stella showed him to be a man who looked out for his own interests, and surely those of his young brother as well. Whoever was performing the mischief, he hadn't much longer to do it.

I saved the most important of my concerns for the last. I still had not been in touch with my father, nor done much to free him. I wrestled with possible courses for some time. When I looked at my watch, a lovely little ladies' hunter watch given me by Papa on my sixteenth birthday, I saw I had forgotten to wind it. It still said seven-thirty. The upsetting of my routine had allowed the regular hour to slip by without winding it. There was an elegant long-case clock in the saloon downstairs. I would nip down and set my watch by it. I picked up the lamp by my bedside and moved quietly into the hallway, to avoid disturbing the sleeping house. All was dark and silent, the occupants and servants settled in for the night, although it could not be much past ten thirty.

It was an eerie sensation, to be descending into the pitch blackness of an unfamiliar place, with only a small circle of pale light around me. When I reached the bottom, I had the feeling of a presence there, a human presence. I cannot explain what caused the feeling—I did not actually hear any sound, smell any human scent, or detect any sign of a body or movement. It was that sixth sense of which I am convinced we are all possessed that alerted me to company. I expected to see someone, Mr. Beaudel or a servant, and looked around to see him, so sure was I that I was correct. I got to the clock

48

without encountering anyone, however, and half convinced myself I was wrong, when I detected from the corner of my eye a moving patch of light. The corner of her gown had caught the glow from my lamp. The satin picked it up, caused a shimmering that alerted my eye.

You may imagine my shock to see, sitting in a chair in the dark, Mrs. Beaudel, still dressed in her evening gown, with her hair up. "Oh!" I gasped, as the lamp trembled in my hand, nearly falling. "You startled me, ma'am. Are you—are you all right?"

"All right?" she asked, and laughed warily. "Yes, I am perfectly all right, Miss Stacey. Sorry if I alarmed you. I often come downstairs at night when I cannot sleep. I dislike to disturb my husband. He needs his rest, as older people do," she declared, in a tone of irony. "And what brings *you* downstairs at such an hour?"

"My watch has stopped. I forgot to wind it. I came to check the hour," I said, holding my watch up for confirmation.

"How careless of you. We would not want our dear Lucien in the hands of a careless governess. You won't let it happen again, will you, my dear?" she asked, in a tone not far from menacing, which was an inordinately harsh attitude for a simple oversight. Clearly, Madam did not like to have anyone prowling the house at night.

"I'm sorry, ma'am," I said humbly.

"The time is ten-thirty. You can set your watch in your room. Run along now," she said impatiently.

I did as she ordered, but her surly impatience was a strong hint she was expecting company, and did not want me to see Wiggins. I was still awake at midnight, and did not hear Madam come upstairs.

Hired as a governess, I had of course to perform the duties of one. In the morning I took Lucien to the schoolroom to begin his studies. After lunch, Beaudel came to us and said he was going into Chelmsford, and asked if Lucien would like to go along for the trip. There was obviously some real love for the boy included in Beaudel's makeup. Here was my chance to get to the inn and discover whether Mr. Kirby had arrived in town yet. There was a possibility too of discovering

49

some news of my father. I used the pretext of requiring a few things in town, and received permission to go with them.

We were let off at the main intersection, Lucien and I, to do my "shopping."

"I have to run on down to the jail," Beaudel explained, throwing me into a spasm of curiosity. "It has to do with this van Deusen fellow who stole the diamonds. I shan't be long. I'll leave the carriage at the Stag and Hounds stable, and you can meet me there. About an hour should do it."

I dared not show my face at the Stag and Hounds. "I have to step over to the other inn, Mr. Beaudel. I left something behind yesterday when I packed in a hurry. Would it be possible for us to meet there?" I ventured.

"Certainly. No trouble at all," he answered easily, with no suspicion. "We'll meet there in an hour."

Before doing anything else, I took Lucien off to the Shipwalk, to enquire for Mr. Kirby. "What did you leave behind, Miss Stacey?" he asked as we walked along, alerting me he would have to be got rid of while I performed my real business.

"Just a letter. I'll ask for it at the desk," I improvised.

"Who is it from? Do you have a beau?"

"It's from my father. I had a letter from him which I barely had time to glance at. I want to read it again."

"They will have thrown it out," he advised me firmly.

There was a sweet parlor two doors from the inn. I gave Lucien a few pennies and let him order an ice, while I went quickly to the inn. There was no Mr. Kirby registered, but that did not mean he was not at the Stag and Hounds. My only acquaintance in the town was the inn servant. I asked if I might speak to her, and was given grudging permission.

And when she came to me, I hardly knew what to say. I told her I had become the governess at Glanbury Park, and thanked her for having told me about the position.

"Have you heard anything about Diamond Dutch?" I asked, with only casual interest, mentioning that Beaudel was even then at the jail.

"Not a word. You'll know more about that than we do here, when you meet Mr. Beaudel after his visit. Did they learn where the other governess went off to?"

"No, nothing."

"The servants are leaving there in droves. Who did they get to replace old Norton?"

"Norton?"

"The butler. They must have replaced *him.*"

"Oh, a monstrously handsome young fellow—Wiggins. I thought he would be well known in town. Quite a ladies' man."

"I've never heard him mentioned."

She could not take long from her work, and I could not abandon Lucien for long either, so I went to the sweet parlor and met him. It was necessary to make a few purchases, after claiming that excuse for coming to town, so I bought a yard of muslin and some lotion. Their selection passed the hour until we met Mr. Beaudel.

"What is the news from the jail, Mr. Beaudel?" I asked at once. "Will Diamond Dutch be going to trial soon?"

"Not for a few weeks," he said, which was excellent news for me. "The magistrate is up to his eyes in cases. He could have held a hearing and let van Deusen be bound over for the spring Quarter Session, but he will never budge a step out of his way, old Heffernan."

"Did you see van Deusen?" I asked, wearing a polite face of mild interest.

"No, I had no desire to see him. He had a fellow with him, they told me. His solicitor, I daresay."

I was unsure how much interest I dared to display, but I did ask for the solicitor's name. "I have no idea. Probably someone from London. Willowby is the best solicitor in town, and he would have spoken to me if he were taking the case. Indeed, he is my own solicitor, so I don't expect he could take the case if he wanted. There would be a conflict of interest, you see, Miss Stacey. And what did you two do with your morning?"

"I had an ice, Uncle," Lucien told him. "Miss Stacey gave me the money."

I trembled lest he blurted out he had been left alone to eat it, but he did not.

"That was generous of her. You will be reimbursed, Miss Stacey. We don't want you spending your hard-earned blunt

51

on this rascal." He reached into his pocket on the spot and jingled a few pennies into my hand, which was very thoughtful of him.

While Lucien chattered, I sat wondering what solicitor my father could have hired. We did not have a family solicitor. Our business matters were not large or complicated enough to ever have required one. There was some worry too as to how he would ever be paid. A city solicitor would not come cheap.

Beaudel enquired, as soon as we were inside the door, whether Major Morrison had arrived yet. He had not, but Mrs. Beaudel was decked in the finest array to greet him when he did come. She wore green sprigged muslin, with green grosgrain ribbons laced through the edifice she had erected on top of her head. She looked quite lovely, but too ornate for midday. The hair did not match the gown, and the gown did not match the silken shawl she was in the process of drawing around her shoulders. Each part of the toilette was unexceptionable, but not together, and not all for day wear. I concluded Madam had gained her notions of elegance from fashion magazines, and not from good company.

I believe she was tired of waiting for the Major to come. When I went to my room to put off my bonnet, I saw through the window that she was walking through the park. Strolling I mean, not hastening anywhere. Beyond, in the middle distance, the onion dome of a Chinese pavilion was visible. One sees many such gazebos since our Prince Regent brought them into fashion. This one, perhaps, might prove on closer examination to have an Indian influence, as the Beaudels had some long association with that country. I would take Lucien there soon and examine the gazebo.

Amidst my other concerns was to learn something about Miss Little, the vanished governess. When Tess, the kitchen servant, brought our dinner to the nursery, I undertook to quiz her about this lady, after first sending Lucien off to wash his hands.

"Has anything been heard of Miss Little, Tess?" I asked.

"No investigations are being made, miss," she told me, with a knowing look on her face.

"Surely that is odd!"

"I don't know about that. A girl that got a letter from her beau one day and that was seen walking with him in the park the next, the very day she took off—well, there's not much doubt where she went, is there?"

"She *did* have a beau then. Lucien said she had not."

"She was as close as skin to a lemon, miss. She never said a word about it, but she got a letter, and it didn't look like a lady's fine writing to *me,* though she claimed it was from a girl friend."

"It could have come from a relative, a brother or father."

"Why would a decent relative go sending his note to the back door by a messenger? He'd have it come with the mail, if he wasn't ashamed of hisself. And she didn't have no family either. She made a point of telling us all so."

"I understand Sir Algernon hired her in London."

"He was taken in good and proper. We all were. We thought she was a very nice sort of a girl, but you see how she carried on when she got the chance. She's not a bride is what we all think in the kitchen, miss. Why else would she make a great mystery of it, but that she was ashamed of herself, and so she should be too."

"That is a pity. What have we for dinner?" I asked, to terminate the subject. "Ah, a nice slice of lamb. It should be tender this time of the year."

"So it is, miss. I've had a bite belowstairs, and never tasted lamb so good," she smiled, unstacking the tray and laying out our meal very nicely.

Despite all my problems, I was ready to do justice to it. I expect I inherited my hearty appetite from my father, although I am happy to say I have not inherited that very large, square frame one sees so often in Dutch ladies. My English mother was dainty, small-boned and delicate, which modified my size. I wish I had got her beautiful face as well, but I confess to a broader set of cheekbones than I like. Mama's sable tresses too are bleached to a less opulent brown in me, but at least I inherited her natural wave. Mrs. Farell tells me I am "lively," by which I have come to learn she means pretty. She is kind enough to tell me if I would bother to tone

53

down my pink cheeks with powder and call in a coiffeur to tend my hair, I might nab myself a beau. You may be sure that when I meet a gentleman worth so much bother, I shall do it.

Chapter Six

It was during our dinner that Major Morrison arrived, causing us to jump up from the table for a dart to the window. He traveled in a high style for a retired major. He was perched in a yellow sporting curricle behind a team of matched grays, with his domo—groom or valet or batman—beside him. This means of travel all the way from Devonshire indicated a heavier traveling carriage somewhere between here and there, carrying his luggage. No more than the top of his hat was visible from our window as he drove up to the house. Lucien proclaimed him a bang-up fiddler. He also expressed an intention of going to the stable to examine the prads as soon as he was finished eating.

I went downstairs with him, and learned in the kitchen that the major, arriving at such a gauche hour, had been invited to remain for dinner. Stella would not be behindhand in offering the hospitality of the house to a lone gentleman. I did not get to see him myself for a few hours, when Lucien was called down for his nightly meeting with the family, before retiring.

My first thought upon seeing the major was, *Yes he is a military type, certainly*. An officer and a gentleman. It was an impression I was obliged to alter on both counts before many hours' acquaintance. He was tall, his shoulders held back and his chest expanded, nearly filling the doorway with his body, when he and Beaudel joined us, after taking port in the dining room. He would not have traveled in evening clothes, but wore them then, which indicated that he might be remaining overnight. Glanbury Park was not so formal as to preclude taking dinner in a blue jacket. These thoughts were fleeting. The feature that held the attention, and affirmed in my mind that he was indeed an Army man, was the black moustache and beard, and the closely cropped hair. Such hirsute adornments were not fashionable amongst any but Army gentlemen. Even amongst them, it was a style more favored by the older set, to which Major Morrison could not be said to belong. He was in his thirties, I thought—somewhere in the low thirties.

His walk was measured, precise, very military, as he drew up before us. In fact, he very nearly clicked his heels, like a Prussian officer. I examined his face, that part of it not covered with hair, as Beaudel introduced him to Lucien. His eyes were a very cool, deep gray, and the skin was as brown as tanned leather. "The Peninsula" clicked automatically into place in my mind. My late brothers' friends, who called on us when they returned to England, had such complexions. The major's was perhaps even a shade darker, indicating a long stay in that hot climate. His anatomy was sleek, well muscled and lithe beneath a modestly patterned waistcoat. All this was observed in less time than it takes to tell.

Within minutes, I had in my possession a more interesting fact than any of this. The major, so self-assured in appearance, was ill at ease, nervous. His eyes shifted, darting about the room, to Lucien and myself, and Mrs. Beaudel, and the door, and back to Lucien very frequently. What possible interest could a retired major have in a young boy he had never seen before? The hands too betrayed his agitation. They held

56

a quizzing glass, which he fingered unconsciously. Beaudel, on the other hand, was quite at ease.

"How did you leave Lord Sacheverel? I hope he is well," Lucien said, the perfect little gentleman. "You mentioned in your letter you are acquainted with him."

"He is very well, for his age," the major replied, then turned his attention back to Beaudel. "It was, of course, Sacheverel who told me about the jewel collection. As I am interested in adding to my own few pieces, he suggested I speak to you. Are you, in fact, selling off the collection?"

"Not in the least. I can't think how these rumors get started. It is only a few odd stones that are for sale, Major. I hope you have not come far out of your way on the hope that anything in the nature of the rose Jaipur is for sale."

"No, actually it is the Italian pieces of the sixteenth century that interest me most. Sacheverel told me Sir Giles was keen on the same period, and had some few items."

"They are not actively on the market," Beaudel told him, "but the right price will always be given consideration. As my wife is always telling me, cash will accumulate interest, while the jewels do not. There is something to be said for selling. If you care to make an offer after you have seen them, we can discuss it at greater length. Well, Major, as you are out of uniform, would it be more proper to call you *Mr.* Morrison?"

"I have the local militia group at home under my command, and am still called Major there," he replied, preening his beard in a pompous fashion. He liked his Army trappings too well to part with them, was my own feeling. I made sure we would be hearing tales of his heroism, without too much prompting.

"Is that so? The local militia have disbanded, since Bonaparte is rid of, once and for all."

"There is no hurry to be rid of it," he said quickly. "No hurry at all. There is no saying Boney won't escape again, as he did from Elba."

Beaudel was too polite to dispute this statement, but of course everyone knew a rocky island off the coast of Africa was a far different story from Elba, where Bonaparte was not even held prisoner or anything of the sort.

"Were you ever engaged in battle against Napoleon yourself, Major?" Mrs. Beaudel asked, to give him an opportunity to brag. She knew how to play up to a man.

"I was at Waterloo," he answered briefly. I expected more details of his prowess.

"A stunning victory for Wellington," Beaudel said, mouthing the gospel on every Englishman's lips. "I expect most of your career was spent in the Peninsula."

"Quite, quite. Vitoria, Talavera, Salamanca, Burgos—I was at them all. I was an aide-de-camp to the Iron Duke," he said, in a dismissing way.

"Indeed!" Beaudel exclaimed, sitting up, impressed with this story. We all like to meet one who has actually been on intimate terms with the mighty. "What sort of a man is he?"

While the guest went on with some details of the general's personality and behavior, I regarded him closely. With a brother who had been in the Peninsula, I had followed the campaign more closely than most. When returned soldiers, of whom I had met more than a few, spoke of the Peninsular battles, it was more common to name them in the order in which they had occurred. Talavera, Salamanca, Vitoria—as they worked their way up from the border of Portugal to France. The haphazard arrangement jarred on my ear. Worse, to have thrown in the defeat of Burgos with the victories was such a questionable thing that I began to wonder if Major Morrison had ever been in the Peninsula at all, or whether he were not a stay-at-home major, who paraded his farm hands up and down the village green, playing at war.

I decided to test him, which meant putting myself forward more than a governess might politely do. Our role was to sit back and listen, speaking only if our charge got out of hand. My test must pose a question whose reply required some close knowledge of the Peninsular wars. Burgos seemed a likely subject for the test question. When he began on some talk of taking French prisoners, I asked innocently, "Would you have taken a great many prisoners after a battle such as Burgos?"

"Hundreds of them," he said, waving a hand airily.

This absolutely confirmed in my mind that the man was an impostor. After the defeat of Burgos nearly half the English Army ended up prisoners, whereas the French seldom left many soldiers behind. Wellington had been confused at the reason for finding so few stragglers, and concluded that the French marched more quickly, and kept closer ranks. I rather wondered that Beaudel did not realize Burgos had been no victory for us, but the battle had taken place some time ago, and our defeats always received less publicity than our victories.

If Major Morrison was not a real major, then who was he, and why was he here? I have already indicated that he directed a good deal of attention to Lucien, which is not to say he omitted Mrs. Beaudel from his observation, or myself either. He was a very sharp observer of us all. The hostess could not be accused of outright flirtation, with her husband sitting beside her. She actually said very little, but she managed her heavily-lidded eyes in such a way that before long, the major began directing the better part of his conversation to her. After some interchanges between them, he returned his attention to Lucien.

"So you are the little fellow who owns the Beaudel collection," he said heartily, while his fingers massaged his quizzing glass. "You are pretty young to own a boxful of diamonds and jewelry. I hope you take good care of them."

"My uncle takes care of them for me," Lucien replied, in his foggy little voice that could still surprise me by its deepness. "A man tried to steal some a few days ago, but Uncle caught him."

"That is a shocking thing!" the major exclaimed, looking to Beaudel for confirmation.

With my mind alive to some charade on this man's part, I began to see playacting in every move he made. I took the notion he was no more surprised at the story than I was. He knew it all along. It is not that he did not react strongly enough. Quite the contrary, he overreacted. His gray eyes widened, his brows shot up. The whole performance smelled of Covent Garden.

"I was very surprised," Beaudel allowed. "He was an eminent authority in the jewel world. I had not thought Diamond Dutch would sink to stealing, but he was caught with a few stones in his pocket."

"No better than he should be, I daresay," Morrison said.

I glared at him, the gorge rising in my throat. He lifted his quizzing glass and regarded me for a longish moment, while I stifled my anger, unable to retaliate. Then he turned back to Beaudel. "Were they valuable stones he stole?"

"As to that, he did not have access to anything worth real money. They were not flawless gems, nor very large. Some of the pieces my brother picked up in India for an old song, but very likely *he* did not know that."

"If the foremost diamond expert in the country did not know it, who would?" the major asked, his head at a haughty angle.

For half a moment, I felt it would be possible to like the major. It was an excellent point. If my father were to steal, which he never would do, he would not bother to pick up a handful of flawed or small stones worth very little. He soon rattled on to earn my disgust.

"Of course if he were short of blunt, he might very well sink to stealing baubles. Well, he *did* do it, so there is no point in discussing the matter. Shall we have a look at the Italian jewelry now, sir? I shall return tomorrow to see them in the light of day, of course. I hope it will not be cloudy. How about it, Lucien? May I see your jewels?" he asked, turning to the boy.

"You will have to ask my uncle," Lucien told him.

This was not necessary. Beaudel was already arising to go for the key, while his wife took advantage of his absence to roll her eyes at the major, and he took advantage of the opportunity to compliment her on her appearance, finding it eligible to tell another man's wife he was surprised to discover *one* quite unsuspected jewel at Glanbury Park.

It was Lucien who called them to order, in his own inimitable and blunt way. "Aunt Stella always looks well when we are having company. She dresses up for hours."

"Children should be seen, and not speak unless spoken to, Lucien," I felt obliged to tell him, but my heart was not in it.

"People hardly ever speak to me when there are adults about," he replied.

The major engaged him in some pleasant nonsense until Beaudel returned, then we all went along to the study for

60

another view of the collection. I was not specifically invited, but as Lucien went, I tagged along. The jewels I have already described. The major examined them with the keenest interest, and a few comments indicating that he knew what he was talking about. The old Italian necklace he was particularly interested in. He was marvelously impressed with it, and hinted without asking outright why it was for sale. Beaudel repeated he was not actually eager to sell, and pressed the major for some idea of what price he had in mind.

"I will have to have my man examine it thoroughly," he said, to evade a quotation. It was a common practice for each party to push the other for the first bid. "He should arrive from London tomorrow. A pity to put him to the bother when Diamond Dutch is within a stone's throw of your front door, but I don't suppose they'd let him out."

"I wouldn't let him inside the house if he were allowed out," Beaudel said sharply.

"Quite right," the major said, in his curt, military way, that reeked to me now of playacting. "If you have any other such pieces, I would be interested in seeing them as well."

Mrs. Beaudel urged her husband to show him the sapphire, which Beaudel did, but unwillingly. She wanted the major to admire all the various pieces, but whether this was to have a chance to talk to him, or in hopes he would want to buy, was not quite clear to me. When the display was finished, she rang for Wiggins and ordered tea. You never saw a more proper butler than Wiggins, nor a more uninterested mistress than Mrs. Beaudel. Morrison was not the only actor in the house.

Lucien and I were not included in the taking of tea. We went upstairs and I put him to bed, with all the little rituals established the night before. I did not learn by what sequence of events the major was invited to remain overnight, but when footfalls were eventually heard coming up the stairs, there were three pairs of feet, and a lady's voice pointing out a guest room to Major Morrison.

Knowing the lady's predilection for nighttime meetings belowstairs, I was afraid to roam myself. Just what I might hope to discover was unclear besides, although I was curious to rifle Mr. Beaudel's desk, on the off chance of finding some piece of incrimination. Before many more nights, I planned to follow Mrs. Beaudel and find out just what it was she and Wiggins did belowstairs, other than make love, that is. When at last the house settled down to silence, I tiptoed to my door and placed my ear against it, to learn whether Stella left her room. Hearing nothing, I opened my door and went quietly into the dark hallway. No light came up from below, but there was a line of illumination visible beneath the door of the room given to Morrison. Glancing at Lucien's room, I noticed that his door was open. I went back for my lamp and went in, to see that his bed was empty. He was not in the room.

The most terrible misapprehension came over me, all in a flash. I took the idea someone was planning to harm him. Kidnapping, even murder did not seem too farfetched, there in the dark, thundering silence of the night. I had to tell Beaudel, of course. I turned down the hall to do so, past Morrison's room. As I passed, I heard a snicker of suppressed laughter within, Lucien's laughter. I did not know whether I was more relieved, or shocked, or angry. I was extremely agitated in any case, and went in that state to the major's door and knocked sharply. I blame my next inexcusable step on my state of nerves. I went barging in without waiting for anyone to bid me enter. I might have been faced with the major in any state of dishabille, but was confronted with no more than him in shirt sleeves. His jacket was cast aside, his boots kicked against a wall, while he himself was sprawled on the bed, playing with toy soldiers.

"What is going on here?" I demanded at once.

"A reenactment of the Battle of Waterloo," the major answered, regarding me with a pair of devil-may-care eyes. All traces of the military gentleman were abandoned. The slovenly disarray of his garments spoke clearly of an unfamiliarity with Army life. I remember my surprise to see in what tidy form Richard kept his room on the few occasions we had the pleasure of his company, after he had taken his commission. His batman was partially responsible, but an officer would be sure his batman kept the place neat.

"A defeat, or a victory?" I demanded, remembering Burgos.

"Oh, a victory. We are being the English, of course," he

answered, unaware of my irony. "Did you take me for a Frenchie?"

I ignored him. "Lucien, what are you doing out of bed at this hour?" I asked angrily.

"I am playing soldiers with Major Morrison. He invited me to."

"At eleven-thirty at night?"

"It was only eleven when we started," he told me, with a conspiratorial little grin at his newfound friend.

"Never volunteer any information under interrogation," Morrison cautioned him, with a playful quirk of his brows in my direction.

I could see no good reason why this visitor should be at pains to insinuate himself with Lucien. At that moment, I could see no bad reason either, but such an unusual act must have some explanation.

"Go to bed at once," I ordered.

He looked to see if the major would countermand this order. "She's the boss," Morrison told him ruefully.

"A girl can't be a boss," Lucien countered, regarding me as though I were less than nothing, though he did begin gathering up his soldiers.

"You'll learn better as you grow older. Women are *always* the boss," the major told him, as he got lazily, and belatedly, to his feet, a leery light in those gray eyes.

"Don't be angry with the boy. It is my fault," he said.

"Did you awaken him at eleven o'clock at night to invite him to play?"

"Of course not. We could both have waited till morning for such a rare treat. I merely opened his door to see him, and as he was awake, he showed me his soldiers."

I stared, incredulous, at his having gone down the hall after being shown his room by the Beaudels, to look at Lucien. "I like children," he added lamely.

I continued to stare. The excuse was unacceptable, and he knew it. "The fact is," he continued, "I had a son myself, who would be Lucien's age now, if he had lived. A little older. He died while I was in Spain. I never knew him at this age. I hope you can forgive me."

He looked at Lucien with a sad little smile as he spoke.

How quickly I had been put in the wrong. I felt a perfect monster, complaining of his behavior, when it had such a grievous reason behind it. "I'm sorry," I said.

."It is quite all right. You could not possibly know. How should you? It was wrong of me to pull the child out of his bed at such an hour. It shan't happen again."

Lucien had his soldiers in their box, and came toward the door. "I will go back to bed now, Miss Stacey," he told me, with great condescension.

"You'd better, before you get me into any more trouble," Morrison said, tousling his head and smiling, with what looked like real affection, at the boy. It softened his harsh face, that smile. I found myself wondering how he would look with a clean shave. He was not as old at close range as I had thought. Or rather, this less martinet-like posture and expression lent a more youthful air to him. I now judged his age to be in the late twenties. He had married young, to have a son Lucien's age.

While these thoughts passed quickly through my mind, he went on speaking to Lucien. "Don't forget you're going to show me your pony tomorrow."

"Don't *you* forget you are going to buy me an ice," Lucien bartered back.

An ice could not be bought closer than at Chelmsford. If the major thought Lucien would be allowed away from home with a virtual stranger, I was sure he was mistaken, but that would be for Beaudel to tell him. "If we can prevail on Miss— ah, Stacey's, is it?—good graces to let you off the leash," the major answered, with a playful, quizzing glance at me. "Do you allow such freedoms, ma'am, or are you not an old enough hand at the job to have established rules yet?"

"Miss Stacey has only been here for two days," Lucien answered for me.

The satisfied air that settled on the major told me as clearly as words that this was what he had been angling to discover. Why on earth did he want to know that? For that matter, how had he come to suspect I was so new at the job?

"That's what I thought," he said cryptically. "Miss Stacey is much too young to have been here longer than two days."

A guilty flush suffused my face. What did the man know?

"What a pair of ruffians we are, Lucien. We have set the young lady to blushing. One would think a London lady would be more accustomed to bantering."

"Miss Stacey isn't from London. She is from Norfolk. Her papa is a doctor," Lucien answered.

"Is *that* what she told you? Then of course it must be true. We gentlemen never question the word of a lady. Or hardly ever. Good-night, Miss Stacey. I hope you sleep well. I look forward to seeing you again tomorrow. I am sure you and I will have a great deal to talk about."

"She mostly likes to talk about 'rithmetic," Lucien warned, as he went out the door.

The major bowed us out, and stood with his arm against the jamb, smiling as we hastened off. I am convinced no officer would stand so casually. Their bones or joints stiffen up so that they stand like wooden men, even when waltzing. Oh no, this major was no real veteran, but who, and what, was he?

Chapter Seven

One can never expect to sleep well in a strange bed for the first few nights. Add to that the number of problems I had to consider, and you will have some idea how long I lay wide awake, staring about the room until the light spots of pictures on the wall became visible. I listened for sounds of traffic in the hallway, and heard none. My last trip to the window to read my watch by the light of the moon told me it was three. I thought about Stella, and found it odd she had waited until she was nearly thirty before marrying. Such a pretty woman must have had many offers. It was odd too the major had said no single word all evening to indicate he was a married man. It had come as a shock, his saying he had had a son. Yet his affection for Lucien was the least contrived part of his behavior.

On my three-o'clock trip to the window, I made the error of leaving the curtain open, so that I was roused by the sun streaming full in my face at six-thirty in the morning. I wondered if Papa could see the sun, in his cell in jail. I was making remarkably little progress in getting him out. At seven, I abandoned all thought of sleep. I arose, washed and dressed myself to face the day. Lucien was still sleeping, so I left him and went to get a shawl for a morning stroll. There were no servants about, but the front door had been unbolted, and the tantalizing aroma of coffee wafted on the air. The air was brisk as I set out across the park, choosing the pavilion for my destination.

As I approached it, only the upper half was visible, for an ilex hedge ran down the side nearest the house, protecting some flower beds from the wind. It was open, with pretty ogee arches, gilt-trimmed, but the silhouette in one of the arches soon distracted my attention from architecture. There, framed like a picture, stood Major Morrison, flirting to the top of his bent with Mrs. Beaudel. I gasped in astonishment, for while I was not close enough to hear any words, I could see the bantering, bold smiles they wore, could see her head cocked at a coquettish angle. Soon the nature of their rendezvous was confirmed. While I peered through the bushes, he pulled her into his arms for a long embrace. And she, the brazen trollop, put both her arms around his neck, running her fingers up and down through his hair. I was never more shocked and disgusted in my life. Two married people, out carrying on like the lowest mortals on earth.

I fought a strong impulse to make my presence known, but a sober second thought deterred me. Their passion showed no signs of abating, and as I took no pleasure in observing it, I turned and scampered back to the house, to wait for Lucien to stir. From my window, I saw, about fifteen minutes later, Mrs. Beaudel return alone through the park. There was no way of knowing where the major had slunk off to. Down to the dairy barns perhaps, for a quick seduction of one of the dairymaids.

Or was there more than lovemaking going on at the gazebo? Had those two known each other before? It was difficult to believe they had reached such an intimate footing in one evening, under the very eyes of the lady's husband. Surely their meeting that morning had been arranged in advance.

67

Whatever the major's habits, I could not believe Stella Beaudel normally hauled herself out of bed at the crack of dawn.

Soon Lucien was up, ready for his breakfast. At some point in the interval, Morrison had returned to the house and eaten. He loomed at the schoolroom door just as I was opening the reader to begin lessons.

"Beginning your favorite subject so soon, Teacher?" he asked, stepping in, and smiling at us. "Hallo, Lucien. Have you had any luck in gaining freedom from classes for our little trek into Chelmsford?"

Lucien made an unintelligible sound of delight, while Morrison began his persuasions. "Such a lovely day. You will welcome the respite yourself, Miss Stacey."

With such an uncertain character as the major wore, I had no intention of letting Lucien accompany him. "I'm afraid we work, sir, rain or shine," I answered, not looking up from the reader. "I can't let him go for any reason."

"What better reason is there than an ice treat? I personally would walk a mile for an ice. We had no such delicacies in the Peninsula."

"They are by no means rare here. We have a great deal of work to do."

"At six years, Lucien also has a great deal of time in which to do his lessons. A couple of hours can be spared to me."

"What of your associate who comes today to look at the jewelry? Should you not be here to meet him?"

"Certainly I should, and shall. He arrives at two. We will be back long before that."

Lucien yanked at my arm, urging me on to accept the offer, but I shook him off. A youngster didn't know what was good for him. I trusted Beaudel would put a stop to the idea, and resorted at last to using his name to squelch Morrison. "You will have to have permission from his guardian. I cannot think he will let Lucien go off with a stranger."

"I am no stranger to Beaudel. My letter of introduction from Lord Sacheverel has convinced him I am not a scoundrel who abducts youngsters. Perhaps you would care to see it for yourself, ma'am?" he asked, with an ironic smile, as he reached into his inner pocket. My lack of interest in seeing it was apparently evident on my face, as he never did extract

68

the letter. "Naturally I have got Beaudel's permission, before suggesting the scheme to you," he continued. "Come along, Lucien."

Lucien leapt up, knocking over his chair in the process. The two walked out the door, the major forgetting to throw his shoulders back like a soldier, and Lucien forgetting to pick up his chair. I stood helpless, watching them go. Minding Lucien was only my secondary reason for being here, but I still felt culpable to see him go off with a suspicious character. Miss Little had already vanished. Who was to say we would ever see Lucien again? It even flashed into my head the major could be the mysterious "beau" who had carried off the governess.

I flung down the reader and went to Beaudel's study as fast as my legs could carry me. "Major Morrison is taking Lucien off to the village!" I exclaimed, when I was admitted.

Beaudel smiled at my urgent tone. "I know he is, Miss Stacey. I should have told you I gave him my permission."

"But we don't know a thing about him! How can you trust him?"

"I know all about him. He has a letter from Sacheverel. He is a highly respected gentleman. You must not bother your head about it. Indeed he is quite a hero."

"I don't think he was ever in the Peninsula at all," I blurted out.

He laughed merrily. "With that tanned complexion! I should say he was. He was honored for his part in the Battle of Vitoria. And he will soon be better known in England as well. You'll never guess where he goes when he leaves us, Miss Stacey. To Brighton. He is invited to pass a few weeks with the Prince Regent at his Brighton Pavilion. Sacheverel mentions it."

Beaudel must have read some doubts still on my face, for he said next, "There is no possibility the letter was forged. It had Sacheverel's seal on it. As far as that goes, I have known of the Morrisons for years. Ever since my brother married Sacheverel's daughter, I have been hearing the name mentioned, always with some good word of them."

I could think of no more protests. "I see," was all I said. My heart was still unconvinced, and the most damning thing about the man, I could not say. I saw him making love to your wife. How could I tell this poor infatuated old fool that? I couldn't. A womanizer would be unlikely to harm a boy in any case.

Just as I was about to leave, defeated, Beaudel suggested, "Why don't you go with them, if you are uneasy? I appreciate your concern for the boy. It speaks well for your interest in your duties. I know Lucien is in good hands when he is with *you*."

"That's a good idea. Thank you," I said, and dashed above for my bonnet, before the carriage should get away without me.

I felt every bit as welcome as a swarm of midges when I hailed them up, just at the front door, as the yellow curricle clipped towards the driveway. "What is it? What's the matter now?" Morrison asked impatiently, drawing his nags in.

"Nothing is the matter. I'm going with you."

"You can't, Miss Stacey. This is a two-seater," Lucien pointed out smugly, and with some cause too.

"Why?" Morrison asked bluntly.

"Mr. Beaudel wishes me to go," I replied, giving a little more strength to Beaudel's wishes than was quite truthful.

"This is nonsense!" For about thirty seconds, I thought he was going to whip the horses into motion and leave me standing in the drive, but after a hasty battle with himself, Morrison invited me, very unenthusiastically, to crowd myself in if I could. It was a close squeeze, but I meant to go if I had to put Lucien on my knee. It would have been more comfortable than the way I went, hanging half off the seat's edge, clutching the side of the carriage for dear life. I know Lucien could have moved over more if he wanted to, but he was offended with me. He scowled and glared the first mile of the trip. None of us said a word. The "pleasure" trip was off to a flying start.

When the two of them tired of being angry, they relaxed and began to discuss the outing. "We have got two cannons from Waterloo mounted in the square in town," Lucien told the major. "I'll show them to you."

"English or French?"

"Oh, English. We would not want French cannons. You

70

can sit on them to have your ice. I often used to sit on them when Miss Little took me into town. We'll each sit on one," he added, with a "so there" glare at me, depriving me of the thrill. "I *liked* Miss Little. *She* never used to come into town with me and Algernon when we didn't want her to."

I gazed off across an apple orchard, refusing to take umbrage at the boy's childish taunts. "Who lives there, Lucien?" I asked, as though he were not furious with me.

"Nobody," he answered mutinously. "Nobody lives in an orchard but birds. And worms."

I turned to rebuke him, but as Morrison's lips were twitching, I rephrased my reprimand. "I have not usually found you so dull," I remarked blandly. "Being in a snit has robbed you of your wits."

"If you mean who lives in the house, why didn't you say so?"

"I thought even a six-year-old child would be clever enough to understand my meaning."

"I am not a child."

"Excuse me. A six-year-old *man* is what I meant, of course."

"Why don't you two chil—you two stop squabbling?" Morrison suggested. "There is nothing else for it. We are stuck with her, Lucien. Let us just pretend she is welcome." The rudeness of his speech was mitigated by a smile to me over Lucien's head.

"If we pretend that, she will want to come again," my charge pointed out.

"A good point, but if she is like most ladies of my acquaintance, she will be into the shops the minute the carriage stops, and we men can go and sit on the cannons in peace."

"There wasn't much point in Miss Stacey's coming then, was there?" the child asked.

"She came to protect you. Miss Stacey mistrusts me for some reason," he answered, lifting a brow in tacit request for an explanation.

"Mr. Beaudel suggested it," I said.

"He did not suggest it when I asked his permission. I wonder where he got the idea. Never mind, Miss Stacey, you are welcome as the snow—er, flowers, in May."

71

"I begin to wonder what you two had in mind, that you take so much exception to my company."

Lucien looked at me with his sly eyes, but said not a word. "Man talk," Morrison answered.

"Please remember the man's age."

The trip was not a great success, but at least Lucien was protected. From what, I am not at all sure. I do know that various attempts were made to be rid of me. Ribbons, perfume and bonbons were suggested as awaiting my pleasure in the shops. There chanced to be benches as well as cannons in the town square. I occupied one of the former, within view of the cannons, on which Morrison and Lucien sat, eating their ices. Morrison ordered three very large ones, and in revenge for the insults endured, I let him get the three in his hands before telling him I did not care for one.

"Lucky me. I get two," he said, with no ill-nature. He contrived to keep the pair of them from melting and destroying his waistcoat.

Their talk was not audible to me, a few yards away on the bench, but it appeared harmless. They laughed, seeming easy with each other. Lucien was given something, which made me open up my eyes, but in a moment he gave it back, and Morrison slid it onto his finger. He was only showing the boy his ring. No harm in that. When they were finished eating, there was some talk as to what we should do next.

"Let us take a walk down that way," I suggested, pointing in the direction of the jail. My goal, of course, was to try for a look at Papa as we passed.

At the Shipwalk, Morrison left us for a moment, to see if his associate had arrived from London. Thorpe was the man's name. My father had a wide acquaintance with the gem community, but I was relieved to hear the man coming was unknown to us, and so would not reveal my identity. Mr. Thorpe had not arrived yet, and I did not see my father looking out of any window at the jail. After our walk, we returned to the curricle for the drive home.

Mrs. Beaudel was strolling in the park when we got there. Morrison let me down at the front of the house, while he and Lucien took the horses around to the stables. Mrs. Beaudel accosted me at once to inquire where we had been, which I of course told her. She questioned me closely as to the reason for the trip.

"Just a treat for Lucien, I believe. He likes children."

"Bah, why should he?" she asked, with a suspicious glance from those muddy-green eyes.

"I expect Lucien reminds him of his son."

"His son!" she exclaimed.

"Why yes, he is married, like you, Mrs. Beaudel. Did you not know it?" I had the pleasure of asking. She glared in open hostility.

"Of course I knew it," she answered. "I did not know he had a son, however."

"His son is dead," I told her, then turned and went into the house.

I had either learned something, or added another problem to my growing store. I did not think Mrs. Beaudel had a notion in the world Morrison was married. Her shock was easy to see, and therefore I did not think they had been acquainted before this trip. On the other hand, Morrison had no great affinity with the truth. He might have invented a son, and perforce a wife, to give him an excuse to seek Lucien's company. But why should he do anything of the sort? I had no idea, except that it *did* seem to give him genuine pleasure. What manner of man was this, who made love to his host's wife before breakfast and entertained his charge after, both with equal enthusiasm and enjoyment? I could not but wonder what he would tackle before nightfall. I was not long in learning.

Chapter Eight

Lucien and I got down to some real work in the schoolroom in the afternoon. High time too! Mr. Thorpe apparently arrived and examined the jewelry, although I did not see him. Beaudel came to the schoolroom and told Lucien about it.

"Major Morrison wants to buy your Italian necklace," he said. "He has offered five thousand guineas for it. Mr. Thorpe, a great expert, feels it is a good price. Do you want me to sell it, Lucien?"

The absurdity of asking a child such a question was obvious, and some sign of it must have appeared on my face. Beaudel undertook to explain it. "My plan, Miss Stacey, is to set up a school fund for my nephew. It costs a great deal to send a chap off to Eton or Harrow, you know. Something will be sold, and I feel I ought to do it now, while I have a good offer. My feeling is that as good, firm offers are received, I shall sell off the collection. You never can find a buyer with cash when you need money."

"As long as you are sure the price is fair. Should you not have your own expert—a second opinion?"

"They were evaluated when Sir Giles sent them home. Perhaps I ought to have Love and Wirgmans do it again, bring the price up to date, as it were. Yes, that sounds a sensible course. I'll do it."

"You will have an evaluation before you sell to Morrison?" I queried.

"I doubt the major would be willing to wait so long. And he has the cash. That is a good point."

There was little to say to so indecisive a man. "I like Major Morrison," was Lucien's childish comment.

"Liking is no reason for striking a bad bargain, Lucien," I advised, hoping Beaudel would heed me.

"Oh it is not a bad bargain. It is more than Sir Giles paid for the thing. I expect I should sell, but I like to talk it over with Lucien. He is the owner after all. I am only the custodian."

"It is not an easy job," I sympathized, as he wore a heavy frown.

"A troublesome task. I wish my brother had left it in Sacheverel's hands, but he is too old. And his sons are busy gentlemen—involved in politics and so on. I am the one with time to spare for it. I shall dump it in Algernon's lap all the same, when he comes of age and returns to his estate. I fear he is a bit young yet."

I was surprised to discover, when I took Lucien down that evening for his visit, that Morrison had left.

"Where is the major?" Lucien asked, scanning the room for his favorite.

"He is in town, putting up at the Shipwalk with Mr. Thorpe, awaiting our decision about selling," Beaudel replied.

"Why didn't you ask him to stay here?" Lucien demanded at once.

A quick little look of animosity passed between Beaudel and his wife. It was unknown whether the husband suspected what had been going on, or the two had come to cuffs over some other aspect of the major's visit. A definite chill was in the air in any case.

"We are not running a hotel," Beaudel answered sharply.

"He has Thorpe with him now. We cannot put up every person who comes to town."

"Is he coming back?" Lucien asked.

"Certainly he will be back. The matter of the sale is not finalized."

"Let us have a hand of cards," Mrs. Beaudel suggested. She directed her remark to Lucien, but I was included. We played for half an hour, during which time it was plain the lady was in a pucker. She was in such ill-humor she robbed the game of any fun for Lucien. I took him upstairs early that evening, as the company below was so inhospitable.

"I don't have to go to bed yet," he pointed out, as we escaped.

"I'll read you a story first, or we can talk, if you prefer."

"Miss Little used to talk to me all the time. More than *you* do," he charged.

"What did she talk about?"

"Everything. Whether I was happy, and all sorts of things. I was very happy after she came."

"Were you not happy before?"

"At first I was happy with Uncle Charles. After he got married to Aunt Stella, the servants became angry. But Aunt Stella got rid of them and hired nicer ones. Then just when we got happy, Uncle Charles became sad, and sometimes mad. I think he is angry with Aunt Stella tonight, don't you?"

"A little peeved, yes."

"He doesn't want her to have any fun. She told me so, and that's why they fight. She fights with Wiggins too. I used to see them go into the writing room and close the door. Sometimes they'd fight, but Aunt Stella doesn't mind fighting with him, because she likes him, you see."

"What does she fight about with Wiggins?" I pressed on, taking advantage of his talkative mood.

"It was something to do with her moving to Uncle Charles's home, after Algernon comes back here. They will be leaving then, because of Algernon fighting with Aunt Stella. Maybe Wiggins doesn't want to go away with her. I don't know. I couldn't hear very well."

This was interesting, but not terribly informative. I already knew she did not treat him like a butler. Soon Lucien

76

changed the topic to some gift Morrison was going to buy him. When at last it was time to tuck him into bed, he apologized for his morning's burst of anger with me. It was just that he and the major had planned a man-to-man sort of a morning, and my coming along spoiled it. I apologized for being such a spoilsport, and was forgiven with the magnanimous rejoinder that I was not really a marplot, only a peagoose.

I was coming to feel rather like one. I had been here for three days, and had nothing for my troubles but suspicions, and suspicions besides that had no immediate bearing on my father's position. Mrs. Beaudel's various dalliances and fighting with everyone were despicable, but unless they led to stealing the diamonds, it was none of my concern.

Time was pushing at my back. I was on thorns to be doing something positive to free Papa. When I heard Beaudel ascend the stairs to bed, I listened closely for an accompanying, lighter tread. Hearing none, I assumed his wife had remained to bicker or flirt with Wiggins. Or possibly to plan with him further depradations on Lucien's diamonds, of course.

I had to go down and spy. Putting it off was getting me nowhere. If caught, explaining my presence below a second time late at night would be difficult. I wondered then whether I might not slip around outdoors and peek through the windows. There was a walk-out platform with a guardrail at the end of the corridor. The servants shook out their dustmops and cloths there, though its true function was more likely a fire escape, as it had a staircase descending to the garden below.

I tiptoed silently to the door at the hall's end, opened it, and slipped out into the chilly night air, where the black sky arced above, with the moon and an occasional star giving a minimum of light. The wind caught my hair and skirts, whipping them about. I was sufficiently familiar with the geography of the house to know I must make a half-circle from the staircase around to milady's room. The grass was damp underfoot, wetting my slippers.

And after all the bother, there was nothing to be seen when I got there but the pencils of light that crept out from the edges of the drawn curtains. I knew someone was in the room, but could neither see nor hear a thing, unless I went inside and resumed my prowling there.

It was mere chance that dictated my continuing around the house, instead of returning to the fire stairs by the way I had come. The distance was equal either way. That random choice proved the most fruitful move I had made thus far. The curtains were drawn in some rooms. In Beaudel's study they were not, and through the blackness, for the room was unlit, I perceived the surreptitious movement of a lantern. It was not the purposeful movement of a man going to a known, preordained spot. No, it was a hesitant, exploratory kind of jiggling about. The flame swung in half-circles, this way and that, as though looking for something. I stood watching, with a nervous churning in my stomach.

I knew I must creep closer to see who held the lamp. It certainly was not Beaudel, behaving so stealthily in his own study. In my mind, I had a fair idea who the intruder was. It was Wiggins, either with or without his mistress, snooping about the room for something. They had had time to nip around from her writing room. The "something" was soon pinpointed, in my mind, to be the safe.

You may imagine my amazement when the first face I saw reflected in the glow from the lamp was Lucien's. A mere child, and one besides who was supposed to have been asleep long ago. I soon realized it was not he who held the lamp. The level of it was too high, and besides he was too far from the light, more than an arm's length away. He was pointing here and there, to cabinets and shelves, directing the holder of the light to various spots. The lamp swung suddenly to the left, and showed me a harsh-featured face, the bottom half of which was covered in a beard. The major's efforts to ingratiate himself with the child were clearer now. It must surely be the first time a thief had sought the aid of his victim to locate the property to be stolen.

I took an involuntary step closer to the window, then realized the more sensible approach was from indoors. Of course I must call Mr. Beaudel. I was too upset to wonder how I would account for what I had seen. Some excuse would doubtless have occurred to me if necessary. I could have told Mrs.

Beaudel instead; she was closer, but the proper behavior could not be counted on from her.

I ran back to the fire stairs, up them two at a time, giving my shin a nasty bark along the way, and on a metal stair edge too, so painful. I went directly to Mr. Beaudel's room and banged on the door. To my astonishment, there was no reply. I rapped long and hard enough to waken the dead, and still there was no answer. Very well then, I'd stop the major myself. A gun, I needed a gun, or a weapon of some kind.

I possessed none, nor had I the least notion where in the house a firearm might be available. As I darted down the hallway, I remembered Lucien had a toy pistol, fashioned to look very real. I would take it. With this harmless weapon to frighten the major into submission, I ran down the stairway to the office, expecting every moment I would encounter Beaudel, hopefully brave enough to help me. He could rouse up a couple of footmen at least. I encountered no one. Not another soul was to be seen. I walked to the proper doorway, taking deep breaths to calm myself. I flung open the door, leveled the toy gun at the major's chest and said—nothing.

"Good evening, Miss Stacey. Do come in," Morrison said, with a smiling look at the weapon. "Lucien, perhaps you will take your toy gun and run along to bed now. I want to talk to your governess."

"All right, Major," he answered calmly. As he walked to me with his hand out for the gun, he said, "I was wrong, Miss Stacey. You *are* a spoilsport after all."

"Lucien, what's going on here?" I demanded. There was no feeling of fright left in my escapade.

"Me and the major were conducting an operation. You have spoiled everything. As usual."

"Call your Uncle Charles at once. Find a footman to fetch him," I ordered.

"Uncle Charles ain't here. He went into town," Lucien replied.

"I didn't hear him leave his room!"

"Sometimes he sneaks down the back stairs, so Aunt Stella won't know he is going to the tavern."

"Call your Aunt Stella then."

"All right," he said, but with such a cunning little smile

over my shoulder to his cohort that I knew he was not going to do it.

"And close the door behind you, Lucien. Quietly," Morrison added. This was done, with the utmost care, not making a sound.

"I hope you have a good explanation for this, sir," I charged, regarding my foe with what traces of dignity I could rally, after being disarmed by a child.

"I might say the same to you, Miss van-Stacey," he answered, with an arch smile, enjoying the affair.

My breath caught in my throat. How had he discovered my secret? And if he told, I would have to leave, before I was clamped into jail. "Are you not curious to know how I learned the truth?" he asked, in a conversational spirit.

"The truth? Why the truth is that I haven't the least idea what you're talking about. My name is Stacey."

"Ah well, what's in a name?" he asked, with a laughing shrug. "This note I have from Diamond Dutch addressed to his daughter will be of no interest to you then," he went on, drawing a white rectangle from his inner pocket.

I reached out for it, advancing towards him in my eagerness. He lifted it just above his head, with a mocking laugh. "Now, now, it would be improper for you to open Miss van Deusen's letter, Miss Stacey."

I reached higher; he held it higher, until I was nearly in his arms, with both of us in some danger of toppling over backwards.

"All right. You know who I am. I admit it," I said, backing off. "Give me my letter."

"Couldn't we play post office some more? The game was just becoming interesting."

"Please!" I said, my voice rising loud enough to frighten him into complying.

He handed it over, and waited with his arms folded while I tore it open to read the miserable few lines my father had scrawled, obviously in haste, but in his own distinctive hand. "Mickey: Major Morrison is helping me. Do what he asks. Help him if you can, then go home. Say nothing to Beaudel." It was signed with his initials. I looked up to see the major regarding me with a question on his face.

"Well?" he asked.

"You know what is in this note?"

"I know what Dutch *said* he was going to put in it."

"You saw my father? What did he say? When did you see him?"

"To answer your questions: yes, I saw him. When? Late this afternoon. He said he did not steal the diamonds. He also requested me to ask you to return home at once to London."

"Of course he didn't steal them! How is he? Is he well?"

"As well as can be expected, under the circumstances. He is not being starved or beaten, if that is your fear. Till he has stood trial, he will not be treated quite like a criminal. Oh, he said you are under no circumstances to go to the jail. A wise decision on his part. You may imagine the conclusion the law would jump to at once, if they learned you were with him all the while. He seems to have convinced them you went back to London before he went to Glanbury Park, or before he returned to the hotel at least. They wouldn't be too happy to learn your real identity here either."

"They won't learn it!" I said, then had second thoughts at the mischievous look that lit up his face.

"There aren't many of us who could tell them," he agreed.

"If there is any *telling* done, Major Morrison, it will not be all on the one side. In fact, I must tell Mr. Beaudel what you were doing tonight. It is my duty."

"It would be the proper course for you to follow, just as it would be proper for *me* to tell him who *you* are. Point non plus, I believe, is the fencing term for the mutual position in which we find ourselves."

I looked at him, measuring the situation. I held up my sleeve a few trumps. He had no reason to know I had seen him with Stella, or to suppose I didn't believe him to be a major, but I would save those cards for another game. "What were you looking for?" I asked.

"Not the diamonds. I know where they are, and you must have observed, from whatever vantage point you were using, that I made no effort to open the safe."

"Yes, but what *were* you after?"

"Something else. I only wanted to *see* something, not to take it."

"Was it the rose diamond, the Jaipur, you wanted to see?"

"I would give an ear to see it, but don't believe he keeps it here in the study."

"It was wrong to use the boy for whatever you're up to. If we are to—to make a sort of pact, Major, I must have your word you will not involve Lucien in anything further."

"I will be happy to oblige, if you will let me use you instead, for the short duration you are here. Your father was supposed to mention your returning to London in that letter. I hope he took time to do it."

"I will not be returning to London till my father is free."

"He mentioned that little streak of the mule. Charming."

"I am determined, not mulish."

"Language is a malleable thing. I had some difficulty recognizing a squat, plain, stubborn woman with mousy hair in you. When I described Beaudel's new governess as a charming girl with big blue eyes and curly chestnut hair, but with a tendency to speak her mind, Dutch was sure she couldn't be you."

"Look again. It's me all right, and your pretty compliments have not made me forget my question. What are you looking for? I can't help you if I don't know."

"Then I shall tell you. I'd like to go over his account books."

"What, you took such a risk only to see his accounts?"

"There's not much risk. Stella and Wiggins are hard at it, and the servants gone to bed. The housekeeper Stella imported has a cunning trick. She rations the candles. That puts the hired help to sleep early. Any idea where the old boy hides his books?"

"No."

"Keep your big blue eyes open. If you plan to stay, that is...."

"That's settled. How will Beaudel's books help my father? He won't have written down that he stole diamonds, or his wife did."

"It will help eventually."

There was a sudden sound of movement in the hallway. As the steps came closer to us, down the hallway, Major Morrison blew out the lamp, and we stood together in the darkness. I expect his heart was beating in his throat, as mine was. I was certain Mr. Beaudel was going to open his study door and catch us out. The steps passed, a light tread, and went upstairs. "Mrs. Beaudel," I whispered, weak with relief.

"I knew it couldn't be Mr. I got him well soused before leaving the tavern. Did you know he drinks?"

"No!"

"Oh, yes. When an elderly gent is married to a dasher like Stella, he either takes to the bottle or beats her, depending on his nature. He often does other foolish things as well."

We were in complete darkness during this part of the conversation. I could not gauge by his tone what foolish things he referred to, but inferred he meant tampering with the collection. My own choice was Stella, but I was not sharing my views with the major yet.

"I must go," I said.

"Mind closing the window after me before you leave?" he asked, very blandly, as though he were suggesting a game of cards, or some perfectly mundane thing.

"Is that how you got in?"

"No, Lucien let me in," he answered, going to the window. His silhouette was perfectly visible, there against the pane of glass, but his moustache and beard hid his lips. Some crinkling at the corners of his eyes made me think he was enjoying himself.

"Shall I tell Dutch you are staying on here for the present?" he asked, as he heaved up the window, making a perfectly wretched squawking sound.

"Yes, if you see him."

"I'll be sure to see him. I am an inspector of jails, Miss Stacey. A perquisite I picked up as a reward for my illustrious military career. I'll tell you all about it soon. Good evening."

He sat on the window ledge, put his legs over the wall, and disappeared from view, but for eight fingertips that clung to the sill. They let go, and a dull thump told me he had reached the ground. I went to lower the window, carefully.

He swept a graceful and exaggeratedly low bow, there in the dim moonlight, one hand on his chest, the other holding his hat, flung out wide. He looked like some gallant cavalier

83

from a picture story book, with his white teeth flashing a smile.

Morrison liked playacting, and he liked women too. It was strange he would ruin his looks with that antiquated beard. Of course it made a good disguise.

Chapter Nine

I learned the next morning that whatever else Major Morrison was, he was rich. He had completed the purchase of the Italian necklace the day before. Beaudel came to the schoolroom to tell Lucien so, and to show him the cheque for five thousand guineas.

"Good. Now I have got my own money," Lucien said.

"You are well off," Beaudel agreed, smiling. His eyes were red, his hand not as steady as a hand should be, after his night's intemperance.

"Has Major Morrison left town?" Lucien asked, voicing a thought that had already occurred to me.

"He stays on for a few days in Chelmsford. He is some sort of a government inspector, looking over the jails in these smaller centers. He will soon be his way to Brighton, to see the Prince Regent."

After a few minutes of talk, Beaudel left. As the weather was so fine, and my student still young, we had some trouble settling down to work. Mrs. Beaudel stopped in to congratulate Lucien on the sale, and to pump him for news. As soon as she learned the Major was in town still, she decided she would run into Chelmsford to do some shopping.

"You two will not want to spend the entire day inside either, Miss Stacey. The last girl used to take Lucien out in the afternoons for some exercise. He likes to go for a walk in the meadow."

"I like to ride my pony better," he pointed out.

"He only walks. You can easily keep pace on foot," Mrs. Beaudel told me.

"Miss Little taught me to play battledore and shuttlecock too. I always beated her," Lucien contributed.

"You shan't beat *me*, sir," I warned him boastfully, though I had never attempted the game in my life.

We both looked forward to the morning's end, for the lovely fresh green trees stirred softly outside the window, and the sun shone invitingly. It was a day to read poetry under a spreading beech tree, to don a wide-brimmed hat and go to a garden party, to take a boat out on a lake, or to walk through the fields with one's beau, if one had a beau.

"We could read just as good outside," Lucien pointed out, when he caught me mooning at the window.

"Just as well," I corrected automatically.

"All right, let's," he said, taking the correction for agreement.

Seeing no possible harm in it, I agreed, but wished first to tell either Mr. or Mrs. Beaudel what we intended. When we reached the downstairs hall, Wiggins was showing a caller into Beaudel's study. There were several callers at the Park, so this was by no means unusual. I told Wiggins what we were doing, and he honored me with an oily, impudent smile.

"A pity you haven't got a little older escort, Miss Stacey," he said. "A pretty young lady like yourself must be bored, here in the country."

"I manage to keep myself occupied," I said haughtily.

He shook his head. "You governesses are all alike. So bound and determined to be ladies you don't have any fun at all. The rest of us servants, the younger ones, are going to a barn dance tonight. You're welcome to come along, if you've a mind to. I just thought you might be dull, that's all."

I decided he was only trying to be friendly, and like Stella, knew no way of setting about it with a woman, except by flirtation. I declined, but thanked him for the offer.

Lucien and I settled under a tree that gave us a view of the house. I was curious to see what callers came, thinking the major might be ingenious enough to find an excuse to come. The only traffic was Beaudel's visitor leaving, very soon after he had arrived, and toward noon, Mrs. Beaudel returned from town, wearing a peeved expression. No luck chasing the major, I deduced.

It was Mrs. Beaudel's habit to take a ride on a showy bay mare after lunch. She pounded off through the park, but I had no way of knowing where she went. The care of her toilette suggested she might be meeting an admirer. On that day, Beaudel came to the nursery and told Lucien he was off to the bank to deposit his check. He tried to look merry, but failed miserably.

With both the master and mistress out of the house, it seemed a good time to look for Beaudel's account books. What they contained that interested the major, I had no idea, but if he was willing to enter the house by stealth, they must be of great interest. When Tess, come to remove the trays, mentioned that the servants were busy setting up the dolly for the weekly wash, I felt I would not have a better opportunity. Even Wiggins was at work, carrying water out. To be rid of Lucien, I sent him to the stable for his pony, then I went quietly into Beaudel's office. His desk top was not littered, as many are. The silver inkpot and a few pens sat in state, with nothing else but a calendar to decorate the surface. It was a double-pedestal mahogany desk, with two rows of drawers. I opened each drawer in turn—none was locked—and found nothing of interest. The material there dated from the days of Sir Giles and his wife. There was a small drawer between the two pedestals. As it was too small to contain ledgers, I had ignored it.

It flew open easily, revealing an untidy welter of business papers of recent date. There were several bills, mostly for items of lady's apparel. Hats, silks, gloves, shoes—the woman was a regular mannequin. A quick estimate sent the sum above the five-hundred mark. Some were marked paid, some not. Rifling toward the back of the drawer, I felt a leather wallet. It was thin, holding only a few sheets of paper. Right on the top was one of such significance I nearly expired. It was an IOU from a Mr. Sangster for five thousand pounds. It was marked paid in full, with today's date. He had used the money from the sale of the necklace to pay his own debts! No wonder he was in such a hurry to get to the bank. He would have to move quickly to get Morrison's check deposited before Sangster made his withdrawal.

The other few pieces of paper were all for redeemed IOUs as well, for lesser amounts. They came to a thousand pounds in all, all dating from the first of the year, a few months after his marriage. I quickly stuffed the papers back in the wallet, returned it to the rear of the drawer, and closed it. I did not continue looking for account books. I felt this was what Morrison had been looking for.

The hall was still empty when I peered through a crack of the door. My next step was to consider how to get this information to Morrison. He was a questionable ally, but my father trusted him, and really there was no one else to turn to. There was no way of knowing when, or even whether, he would return to the Park. I had to go to him, and soon. Getting away from Lucien was the problem. He was even then getting his pony saddled up for a ride, but a groom could accompany him.

What I needed was a good excuse to get into town alone, and a means of conveyance. There was no coach passing by, and it was a long walk—five miles. I weighed the advantages of a toothache against a pain in the stomach, wondering if I would get away alone in either case. Might they not send a servant with me if I claimed to be ill, or worse, have a doctor come to the Park? Dentist then—one had to go to him. As soon as either of the Beaudels returned, I would develop a toothache and arrange a drive into town. Meanwhile, I arranged for a young groom to take Lucien to the meadow.

It fell out that Mrs. Beaudel was the first back. She came striding in from the stable, whipping the side of her skirt with her crop.

"How are you coming along, Miss Stacey?" she asked, with no real interest. "I see your trunks have not arrived yet," she added, with a passing glance at my gown, the same one I had worn since the day I came to them.

"Actually I am not feeling very well," I said at once, to pave the way for my request.

"What seems to be the trouble? You don't look pale."

"It is a toothache that bothers me," I replied, rubbing my jaw and casting a woebegone look on to my face.

"What a nuisance for you. There is nothing so depressing. There is a fellow in town who draws teeth very well. Wiggins had to have one drawn a month ago. Why don't you go to see him?"

"I shall. Would it be possible for me to go this afternoon?"

"Mr. Beaudel has the carriage out. There's a gig . . ."

"That would do perfectly."

"Very well. Go ahead then." She gave instructions, examining me while she did so. "Funny your jaw is not swollen at all," she said.

"I would like to get it tended to before it abscesses."

"You are brave. I always wait till the last possible moment. I dread the dentist so. Will you go right away?"

"Yes, as soon as possible."

"Very well, but you'll have to go alone. The servants are washing today. I *know* they'll destroy my new sprigged muslin," she said wearily, then strode away, her hips swinging saucily. It was a source of continuing amazement to me that Beaudel had ever married this hussy.

I was soon jogging down the road, as quickly as a sway-backed old jade could carry me. It was a farm animal that was hitched to the gig. How I was to get in touch with Morrison was a problem. If he was out inspecting the jail, I would have to leave a note off at the inn. At least I knew he was at the Shipwalk. Beaudel had mentioned it that morning.

I drove there and stabled the gig, then went into the lobby, with the excellent excuse of inquiring for my trunk. To my surprise, it had arrived, and was loaded onto the gig for me, giving me an excuse to linger. The major was not in, so I used the lobby desk to write him my note. Before I had finished,

89

he came dashing across the street, his timing so perfect you would think he knew I wanted to see him.

"What's happened?" he asked at once, in a sharp tone.

"How did you know..."

We walked a few steps from the desk, then I darted back for my unfinished letter.

"I have a fellow on the lookout—a groom at both inn stables—to keep an eye peeled for you. When your trunk came this morning, I hoped you would come in person for it. Now where can we go to talk? Somewhere we won't be seen— my carriage is probably the best bet. I'll bring it around to the front. Wait here." He took my letter, which I was crumpling into a ball. "We don't want to leave any evidence around. Besides, who knows when I'll receive another *billet doux* from you?" He flattened it out and put it in his pocket, so carefully it made me look for a reason.

"If you think you're getting some evidence to blackmail me..."

"What!"

"I didn't sign it."

He shook his head and sighed. "What I was hoping for was something in the nature of 'My dear Major Morrison: I need you desperately....' A man could weave marvelous dreams around such an auspicious beginning." He drew out the paper and glanced at it, frowning at my blunt words. "'Major Morrison: I think I have found what you were looking for.' And they say poetry is dead," he commented, shoving it back into his pocket, much less carefully.

"Hurry up with the carriage. I can't stay long."

"Yes sir," he said, clicking his heels and saluting, with no concern for the few groups standing idly by, watching us.

Within a few minutes I was seated in a very elegant carriage, with the major facing me, demanding to know what had brought me to town. I explained my discovery and my suspicions.

"He made a dart into town to deposit the check. Certainly looks like it in any case," he said. "Good work, Miss Stacey. What was the name on the smaller IOUs?"

"The name? Beaudel's of course. What do you mean?"

"Beaudel was the I. Who was the U?"

"I don't remember." I frowned with the effort to conjure up in my mind's eye those squares of paper, but it was only the largest that I recalled. "I know Sangster was the one he paid off today."

"Better than nothing. You should always remember names."

"What's in a name, major?" I asked, reminding him of his own question, and that we both traveled under an alias.

"What did this Sangster fellow look like?"

"A big, burly man. Middle-aged, wearing a badly cut blue jacket. I hadn't much of a look at his face. His hair was fair, reddish, and his face very pink."

"I'll check around town and see if I can discover who he is."

"What does it matter? The important fact is that Beaudel is using Lucien's money to pay his own debts."

"True, but we have to know why he has these large debts. If they are connected in some way with legitimate estate expenses, we'll look no-how, hauling him up before a judge."

"They are connected with milady's bent for finery."

"He has some blunt of his own, possibly sufficient to keep her clothed in the style to which she wishes to become accustomed. He was certainly providing for himself before his brother died, at least."

"*He* didn't buy six gowns at one time, when he lived alone."

"If he bought even one, I am ashamed of him. Though I doubt two can live as cheaply as one, when one of 'em is Stella. Still, over five thousand pounds in half a year.... That's a lot of gowns."

"Since he drinks, maybe he gambles too, and loses."

"Quite possibly."

"What should we do about it?" I asked eagerly, wanting to terminate the business, for my father's sake.

"We wait, and keep looking," was his highly unsatisfactory answer.

"My father..."

"Dutch is all right. I am keeping him supplied with life's necessities, and even a few of its luxuries."

"The greatest luxury he wants is to be able to work. What will it take to clear his name? I thought if we could prove Beaudel is a thief, it would go a long way to proving Papa

91

is innocent. It would be *his* word, a man of integrity with plenty of people to vouch for it, against that of Beaudel, a proven thief."

"We haven't proven it yet. Be patient. He is the executor of the boys' estates, remember. Even if he's guilty, it would be possible to fudge the books to show the money went into estate business. He might be, or at least *say* in the books that he is, borrowing money from Lucien to loan Algernon. Repairs and renovations of a large estate can run into thousands. Not that I have actually seen any evidence of these major overhauls."

"There's not a single repair or renovation going on at the Park. I cannot imagine what it is you're looking for."

"I have the feeling that when I discover it, I shall recognize it. I am a great believer in instinct. The little hindrance is that I haven't a notion what I am looking for."

"We differ there. I know what I'm looking for, and we're not looking for the same thing at all, *Major* Morrison. Your first priority is not freeing my father, clearing his name of this infamous charge."

"I confess it is not my *first* priority, but as it will surely follow, I consider we are working towards the same end, *Miss Stacey*," he replied, stressing my assumed name, as I had emphasized his own title.

The look that passed between us was closer to animosity than cooperation. "I don't see why I should trust you," I said, frustrated that my discovery had led to so little.

"I could say the same, with perhaps more reason," he pointed out. "The diamonds *were* discovered in your father's pocket after all."

"Not all of them!"

"True, but then *your* pockets were not searched, were they, Miss van Deusen? I don't know what you can possibly accuse *me* of."

"Well upon my word, if this doesn't beat all the rest! You come *pretending* to be a soldier, dressed up in costume whiskers, you seduce Beaudel's wife, you coerce a child into helping you break into the house by bribing him with treats, you——"

"*Pretending* to be a soldier?" he asked, his gray eyes widening. "My dear masquerader, I could show you scars! Lucien quite *begged* me to come visit him, and as to what you no doubt consider the more heinous crime—well, it would be ungentlemanly to imply for a single moment the lady was anything but averse to my attentions, so I shan't bother to imply it. She did not *have* to meet me at the gazebo, however."

"I don't care whose wife you make up to, as long as you keep well away from me. And I don't really mind that you broke into the Park either. What I find utterly disgusting is that you strut about pretending to be an officer. I expect those whiskers you wear are to hide your face from the law for desertion of duty. Any soldier who was actually in the Peninsula would know Burgos was no victory. You must have been living in Bedlam, or Newgate, during those years, to be unaware it was a staggering defeat for us."

Morrison placed his elbow on his knee, his knuckles on his chin and listened politely to my charges. When I had finished, he said, "I really must get hold of a good history of the late war. To be tripped up so easily, and by a *girl* too.... Nothing is really changed, however. We are a pair of masqueraders with no ally but each other in the affair. And let me add," he said with a bow from the waist, "I, for one, would not want any other. Our goals are not inimical, quite the contrary. We are both out to prove the Beaudels scoundrels, so let us work out a more effective campaign than presently prevails. We must have some reliable means of being in touch. I have my little scheme of sticking around on the pretext of inspecting a three-cell jailhouse for the next week or so, which puts my performance on an equal footing with other government employees. We don't want to race ourselves out of a soft job, you know. Is it easy for you to get into town?"

"Easy? It is practically impossible. You have no idea the shifts I have been put to. No carriage, no mount, and no excuse. I cannot have another tooth drawn tomorrow."

"You *didn't* resort to that! Poor girl. No wonder you are in such a bad skin. You must under no condition repeat *that* barbarous——"

"I just told them at the Park I was going to the dentist. I didn't actually do it."

"Thank goodness. Well, since you have no excuse and no
93

carriage, it will be for me to go to you, unless an emergency should arise, in which case you grab the boy and run. To me."

"An emergency? What do you mean? You sound as though..."

"That is precisely the way I meant to sound. If Beaudel should discover we are investigating him, there is no saying what he will be pushed into doing."

"He wouldn't harm Lucien. He is genuinely fond of his nephew."

"I agree, or the boy would not be still with him. Still, there is no saying what a man won't do when he is cornered. A rat will turn and attack his attacker, under enough pressure. I'm not sure a mouse like Beaudel wouldn't do the same."

"It's the cat I'm more suspicious of."

"Why is that?"

I told him about her meetings with Wiggins, the hiring of new servants, and Algernon's dissatisfaction with her running his home. "There was no trouble till *she* landed in at the Park," I concluded.

"I knew all that. Man-talk, while having ices on the cannons. You have not forgotten our delightful outing? My man is at Tunbridge Wells now, looking into her past, and Wiggins's, while he is there."

"Major, are you a Bow Street Runner?" I asked, my heart lifting. "Did Sacheverel hire you to look into this affair?" I could think of no other explanation for what he had just told me.

"I wish I could say yes, since the melodramatic idea appeals so strongly to you. Alas, I must disappoint you, my dear. But I *am* here at Sacheverel's request, if that cuts any ice."

"It does. It's troubled me very much, wondering why you are here."

"I am somewhat encouraged to learn it is only the 'why,' and not the being here itself that troubles you. Even gentlemen with whiskers have feelings, you know."

"I should be getting back."

"Yes, unfortunately you should. It hurts like the devil to have a tooth drawn, but it don't take long. We have not settled on some method of communicating. I don't care much for your style of letter writing," he added with a bantering smile. "Is there some spot near the Park where I could meet you, some place we would not be seen? If Lucien is along, it's no matter."

"He knows who you are, that his grandfather sent you?"

"He knows Sacheverel sent me, but quizzing him for my name won't answer your other question."

"I am to take Lucien to the meadow in the afternoons. We could meet there, unseen from the house."

"What time. Two, three?"

"Let us say two-thirty."

"And on a rainy day? We don't want to lose track of each other, and there's no saying we won't get a week of rain, here in England."

The last phrase hinted at his coming from another climate. He sounded as though comparing it to a different climate, is what I mean. "Unlike the Peninsula," I mentioned, and looked for his reaction, which was only a faint smile.

"I'll tell you what. That metal staircase outdoors at the end of the upper hallway—I'll be there around eleven at night, if I am not in the meadow in the afternoon. It's well removed from the family's chambers. You can meet me there, I take it, without any trouble?"

"I suppose so."

"Don't let your enthusiasm run away with you. You have no romance in your soul—a secret tryst with a dashing stranger. I left out the handsome on purpose, to save you the chore of contradicting it. Let's make it a nightly date, whether we meet in the meadow or not. It will enliven our dull evenings no end."

We were approaching the Shipwalk again, having made a little circuit to one end of town and back. "My evenings are quite lively enough, thank you."

"Is that a refusal? I would happily drive the five miles to see *you,* but to climb a staircase and look in at a vacant window, I'm not sure it's worth it. In fact, I'm sure it *isn't* worth it. I wouldn't have to leave Chelmsford for that sort of excitement. I'll be there. It's settled, starting tomorrow night."

"All right."

"Let yourself out the carriage door. There's no point in our being seen together any more than necessary. If they should hear, at the Park, that you were with me, don't deny it. Better to let them think you're throwing your bonnet at me than the truth. Maidenly blushes should divert suspicion," he added, with a smile not far short of a laugh at my disgust.

Distasteful as the suggestion was, I felt it a wise one. Just as he pulled the check string to stop the carriage, he leaned across to my side of the carriage and put his fingers on my cheek. I was startled at his doing so, as I had not encouraged his dallying remarks. He caressed my cheek a moment, gently, then pinched it hard enough to make me squeal. "There," he said with satisfaction. "That looks more like a face that has undergone a trip to the dentist. Give it another rub before you get home."

"You are very thorough," I complimented him stiffly, and reached for the door.

"Not really. That wasn't what I wanted to do at all."

It was not necessary to ask his meaning. His bold eyes, staring at my lips, made his meaning quite clear.

"There was something else *I* wanted to do too, Major," I said, with a smile, and a modest glance at my fingers.

"By all means, go ahead."

"You're sure you won't mind?"

"I would like it excessively."

"How kind. I want you to find Mr. Kirby for me, and tell him I am very eager to see him. Try the Clarendon Hotel, in London. That is his last known address."

He crossed his arms over his chest and glared. "I will be very happy to oblige you, miss."

"Thank you. You are very kind. See you tomorrow."

I let myself out and called for my gig, happy to see the trunk tied in place. The mood that descended on me as I returned to Glanbury Park was unsettling. I was drifting from my purpose, in going along with Morrison, but was not clever enough to clear father's name by myself. A professional investigator, he had resources that were beyond me to discover what was going on. The man at Tunbridge Wells, for instance, there was no way I could have done that. And if he worked for Sacheverel, he was not likely to run into trouble with the law. But how had he got that tropical tan? Where had he been that he was unaware of the recent great events that had shaken England?

I remembered to give my cheek a rub before entering the house. I told them the tooth had not been drawn after all, but some oil of cloves put in it to ease the pain. I claimed to be feeling much better, to avoid having to go to bed.

Lucien was waiting for me in the nursery. He came to my room with me while I unpacked my trunk and put my things away. "Did you really have the toothache?" he asked, with a piercing look in his shrewd eyes.

"Why would I say I had if I hadn't?" I prevaricated.

"If you were going to meet Major Morrison, I want to go with you. He is my special friend."

"He told me all about it."

"*All* about it?"

"Yes, that Sacheverel has hired him to look after your interests."

A youthful but still very superior laugh greeted my ears. "Is *that* what he told you? What a complete hand he is."

"Lucien, what do you mean?" I demanded, in horrible alarm.

"Don't be startled, Miss Stacey. He is helping me, but what a plumper to have told you—Sacheverel sent him."

For several minutes I questioned him, but learned nothing more. So the major was still a mystery.

Chapter Ten

The evenings were long and dull at Glanbury Park. I never
knew how long an evening could be, until I went there. Our
evenings in London were not gay, mad revels to be sure, but
we had callers, and were invited out, or if we stayed in, we
amused ourselves with cards, or reading, or sewing. Mrs.
Farell was a talented dame with her needle. Here in the
country, country hours were kept. Dinner was over long before dark. There was the short visit belowstairs with Lucien,
but he was in bed at nine. I could have joined the servants
in the kitchen, but the governess, being born a lady, was not
really welcome there. I could almost pity Mrs. Beaudel, who
was as bored as I was myself, with her aging husband sitting
across from her, rustling the newspaper and occasionally
smiling at her from above his spectacles. You could fairly
hear her teeth grind when he did it. It must have been infinitely dull for her. She was stuck with this existence until
her husband should die, whereas I would be released as soon

as I proved my father innocent. One could not condone her carrying on with the butler and casual visitors, but I was coming to understand it.

With no butler to entertain me, I was left with my own indifferent company. My thoughts invariably turned on my situation, and how I could bring the business to a head quickly. It all hinged on proving there was a thief in the house, of course. It now looked as though the thief were Mr. Beaudel, who had, unfortunately, the means to conceal his crime. As this was the case, I wondered how Sacheverel, an old man, and far away, had come to suspect there was anything amiss, and sent Morrison to investigate. It was not the diamonds stuffed into Papa's pocket that had brought him. He had arrived too soon after the event for Sacheverel to have learned of it, and sent him. So there had to be more than that going on.

The star of the Beaudel collection was the Jaipur, the rose diamond. I decided that it was some irregularity with regard to this fabulous thing that had instigated Sacheverel's investigation. There was great secrecy regarding its whereabouts. Papa had not been allowed to see it; Morrison had not seen it. To my knowledge, no one had seen it. One could hardly avoid wondering whether it were around to be seen. It was the Jaipur that Kirby had particularly asked my father to examine and evaluate, so he must have had some reason to suppose it was for sale. The mystery nagged too, that Kirby had never come forward, after asking us to let him know if there was any trouble.

Once I had convinced myself the Jaipur was at the foundation of all the mysterious doings, anything else seemed like time wasted. The thing to do was to discover whether the gem was still in Beaudel's possession at all. Lucien, I knew, thought he still had the stone in safekeeping for his maturity. No point disturbing him by the question. I would tackle Beaudel himself—ask him if I could see it. He would think me forward, which bothered me not in the least. Even if he refused to show it to me, I might be able to judge from his demeanor whether he had it.

The next morning, before speaking to Beaudel, I asked Lucien what the Jaipur looked like.

"It's this big," he said, making a circle with his thumb and index finger. "It's all pink and shiny."

"When is the last time you saw it?"

"At Christmas. Uncle Charles had it out then and showed it to me and Algernon. Algernon asked to see it."

"Had it out from where?" I asked.

"Out of where he hides it, upstairs," he answered, "but I don't know where, exactly, so you need not bother asking me. Miss Little thought he got it from his own room, but *I* think he went up to the attic. You can go to the attic from Uncle Charles's bedroom. It is the only way you *can* go to the tower room. Uncle Charles's room is on the east front, where the tower is. I wish *I* could have it."

"Do you see your rose diamond very often?" I went on, taking mental note of all his answers, for possible future use.

"Usually on my birthday, and at Christmas."

"When is your birthday, Lucien?"

"In September. I will be seven."

September was much too long to wait. I was determined to put my request to Beaudel that very day, but was prevented by the fact of his going away. He received some letter that appeared to upset him, had the carriage harnessed up, and went flying off. His wife, bored with her loneliness, invited Lucien and myself to join her for luncheon.

"Where is Uncle Charles?" Lucien asked, in his grave, polite voice.

"Gone to London, leaving me all alone," she pouted.

"Why didn't you go with him?"

"He is gone on business, and will be back tomorrow."

"What business?" Lucien persisted.

"What a Nosey Parker it is!" she chided. "Your business, Mr. Curiosity. He has gone to arrange some profitable investment for your money."

"He doesn't have to go to London to buy Consols," Lucien told her sagely. "Algernon says you can buy them from an agent in any town."

"Then he must be investing your money in something else, must he not?" she countered, her patience wearing thin. She turned away from Lucien and regaled me with some story she had been reading about a pig-faced lady in London. "Some saucy fellows dressed up a trotter in a bonnet and gown, certainly, and tried to pass it off for a lady," she decided. "Only fancy people being taken in so easily, but it says in the article folks believed it. Well, it doesn't surprise *me*."

"It surprises *me*," Lucien said, wide-eyed with this tale.

"I daresay it surprised the gentleman the pig bit too. They had to send off for a sawbones to tend his wound. What fun they must have in London," she finished, with a wistful sigh.

She was attending a flower show that afternoon. With this to make a *grande toilette* for, Lucien and I were allowed to leave as soon as we had finished luncheon. "Are you ready for your ride?" I asked him.

He was always ready to throw his leg over a pony. "Are you coming with me, or does your tooth hurt?" he asked.

"I'm coming with you."

"Stay home if you don't feel well," he offered, with the instincts of a gentleman. I remembered it had not occurred to his aunt to enquire for my health.

Curious to learn what the major had to say, I went with him. Morrison was there at the appointed spot at the appointed hour. He had come mounted, as his curricle could not negotiate fences and rough meadows. A fine chestnut gelding was chomping the grass beneath a tree, while the major busied himself spreading a white cloth on the ground, and placing two glasses on it. Lucien ran to him to have his silken curls mauled, a form of condescension he did not really like, but he liked the major, so tolerated it.

"You didn't bring a glass for me!" Lucien said, looking at the stemmed glasses on the cloth.

"Wine and sugarplums go very badly together," he replied, producing a small bag of sweets for the boy.

"Are we having a party, Major?" I asked.

"There is no need to deprive ourselves of the amenities of a polite call, only because we are forced to meet outdoors like gypsies," he answered, stepping back to admire his work. "Flowers would be nice," he said consideringly. "I racked my brain to discover some means of transporting tables and chairs, but the lack of a carriage defeated me in the end. Which seat do you prefer, Miss Stacey? The rock is cleaner, I believe, but no doubt the fallen log is softer," he suggested,

101

conning this problem with polite interest, and finally suggesting the rock.

As I had already taken a step toward the log, I sat on it instead, looking about for what was to go into the glasses. "It is chilling, in yonder stream," he said, before I voiced the question. "I have brought a rather good sherry. I hope it meets with your approval." He strolled to retrieve the bottle, and pried out the cork with a penknife.

"There was no need to go to all this trouble," I told him, smiling at the formal manner he had adopted.

"True, we could have drunk it from the bottle, as we soldiers did in the Peninsula, but when a lady is present, one likes to observe the customs." He picked up the two glasses, balancing them between the fingers of his left hand, as he poured with the right. He walked to the log and extended the glasses to me. I took both, to allow him to reinsert the cork and set down the bottle.

"To your very good health," he said, accepting one glass and raising it in a toast. "You are looking charming today," he continued, after taking a sip.

"Thank you. Ought I to say something about the weather now?" I enquired, to show my appreciation of his efforts.

"That usually precedes the requisite compliment on a lady's toilette—no matter what lack of pains her appearance displays," he replied, but with no actual disparaging glance at my toilette. "Shall we rush right along to a query for the health and wellbeing of the family?"

"By all means, for it is of prime interest to *me*. How is my father?"

"He is fine, but you ought more properly to enquire after *my* father, n'est-ce pas?"

"Do you have one?"

"Oh yes, and a mother too. They were married. To each other. I am not the sort of social outcast you think me."

"Uncle Charles has gone to London," Lucien piped in, always wanting to be included in adult conversation.

"We *see* you, Lucien. That is quite enough. There is no need for us to hear you as well," the major said sternly. "In fact, we could see you equally well if you decided to take off your shoes and socks and have a wade in the stream. There are tadpoles in there."

"It will be too cold for him," I countered.

"Not to judge by the temperature of this sherry, it won't."

"Miss Little let me wade a week ago," Lucien told me. This being the case, I allowed him to go, to be rid of him.

"Enough chitchat," the major said, when we were alone. "Did you find out anything of interest?"

"Just what Lucien said—Beaudel has gone to London."

"I knew that already. Unfortunate he didn't take his wife with him. Did you learn why he went?"

"Stella said it was to invest the money you gave him for the necklace, but we know that is not true. Did you learn anything about the man he gave the money to? Sangster."

"The man is a cent-percenter, a professional maker of loans. One trembles to wonder at what percent of interest, when the borrower is in dire need. I approached him, indicating I could use a few hundred pounds, and he mentioned twenty percent. His chief merit, it seems, is that he acts with the greatest discretion."

"So we know Beaudel borrowed money, and didn't want anyone to know it."

"More damning, we know he used Lucien's money to repay the debt. But we *still* don't know why he incurred the debt originally."

"Did you learn anything about Mrs. Beaudel from Tunbridge Wells?"

"My man should be back this evening. These enquiries take a little time. His staying a few days is good news, Miss Stacey. If his questions had not turned up something, he would have been back by now."

"I know she's at the bottom of whatever is going on."

"Is there something other than innate jealousy of another beautiful woman that makes you favor Mrs. for the culprit?" he asked, with a lazy smile.

"I'm not a bit jealous of her. She has a perfectly wretched time. I can almost understand her carrying on with Wiggins and any old scarecrow who comes along. She does it to keep from dying of boredom."

"The old scarecrow who came along thanks you for that flattering interpretation of the matter."

I ignored his attack of pique. "It could take forever to free my father, the way we are going about it."

"Hardly forever. Algernon returns from university very soon. If they mean to try for the real money, they'll be arranging it now."

"By real money, you mean the Jaipur?" He nodded. "I think I know where it is kept."

"Excellent! You *are* a busy little bee. Tell me all about it."

I told him what Lucien had told me. "If Lucien knows it, Stella knows it as well. Why doesn't she just grab it and run, I wonder?"

"Maybe it's hidden so well she can't find it."

"Hmm, and maybe she's waiting for the opportune moment. You think she covered up stealing a few small diamonds by involving your father. There would be a great hue and cry if she just grabbed it and ran, but if she could do it in some manner while there is another suspect around..."

"I see your point. There was no one but family at Christmas and Lucien's birthday, I believe. But he never will show it to anyone. It's not for sale, despite his wife's urging."

"Everything is for sale, if the price is right," he countered, twirling the glass in his fingers, while he looked into the rolling amber liquid. "Yes, I know it sounds cynical," he added, lifting his eyes to quiz me, "but it happens to be true."

"As long as you say every*thing* and not every*one,* I shan't argue."

"Only *some* people are for sale," he agreed.

"Am I to assume you are going to make a ludicrously generous offer for the Jaipur, to get the pot boiling a little?"

"You have a poor appreciation of my mind. A *ludicrous* offer would be suspect. I shall make a reasonably generous offer, no more."

"I got to wondering last night, when I was thinking about things you know, whether he still has the Jaipur at all. It's rather odd he never shows it to anyone."

"How very unflattering! Here I thought you would be thinking of *me.* In the interest of efficiency and saving time,

104

I shall take a look about the tower room tonight and see if I can find it."

"Mrs. Beaudel will be home. You can't very well distract her in your usual manner, when you have to be free to roam the attic at the same time."

"I regret losing such a prime excuse for further dalliance with the lovely Stella, but first things first."

"I'm sure you'll find some other excuse."

"If I don't, she will. She left me off a note at the inn yesterday mentioning a few sequestered rides in the vicinity, and just happening to give the hours when she rode herself. Some ladies are much more ingenious than others in these matters."

"Some ladies don't have to worry about their fathers being in jail."

"Not to worry. I spent a part of the morning investigating security measures at the jail. A clever child could walk out of there without much trouble. In the worst case, we can always take my trusty penknife to his lock, and spring him without benefit of the law."

"Major Morrison, you have the mind of a criminal!"

"Set a thief to catch a thief, as the old saw goes."

This bald admission sent me into a nervous spasm. Who was to say Morrison would not just grab the diamond and run, once he got Beaudel to show it to him? And if he did, my father would languish behind bars until he died.

"Don't be so foolish!" he said harshly, when I stared at him in horror. "Your father trusts me. Would he put you under my protection if he didn't?"

"He hasn't any option."

"*I* didn't put him in jail."

"No, Mr. Kirby did, and I wish I could find that wretched man. Did you have any luck?"

"There hasn't been time. You know my man is at Tunbridge Wells."

"He knew there was something fishy about this business from the start. He told Papa so."

"It is a pity your father hadn't taken some precautions then."

"What could he have done?"

"He could have left his daughter at home at least. I can't imagine his being foolish enough to drag a girl into this mess."

"He would be in a fine pickle if he *had* left me at home! I wouldn't know what had become of him. I'd be worried sick."

"Instead of enjoying the calm, peaceful vacation you are having here!" he snapped back angrily, then relented and offered me another glass of wine.

"No, thank you."

"I don't see any tadpoles," Lucien called.

"You help him, Major. With your lively imagination, you will know where to look."

He sighed wearily and set down his glass. "If I have been rude to you, I apologize. I know you are worried about your father. Believe me, nothing is going to happen to him. You have my word on that."

"The word of a spurious officer and gentleman. How reassuring."

"Only the status of officer is spurious. I *am* a gentleman," he said, with a reckless smile that belonged on a highwayman, or a cutthroat pirate. "And of course my lively intelligence, not imagination, tells me where tadpoles hide. Under rocks. You have to stir 'em out with a stick. Come along, I'll show you."

Feeling no desire to see tadpoles stirred up with a stick, I had another glass of sherry instead, and watched from the rock while he did as he promised, allowing Lucien to use his wine glass to catch some. He poured out the rest of the wine and rinsed out the bottle, so that Lucien might take these trophies home to die in it.

"Eleven at our trysting spot?" he asked, before leaving. "I have nothing better to do. She didn't mention riding at night, in her note."

"All right." I knew he would be looking for the Jaipur, and meant to tag along to see he didn't steal it.

I quizzed Lucien about Morrison on the way home. "How do you come to trust Morrison so much, Lucien?"

"I have a way, Miss Stacey," he answered airily.

"I must know," I insisted.

"He told me women are very curious. I see he is right,"

106

the boy answered, with a patronizing look. I held the line of his pony, and got stuck to carry the tadpoles.

"He told me Sacheverel sent him, and you said that was not true."

"If you must know, Algernon sent him. He has Algernon's ring. He showed it to me. Algernon gave it to him. It is a sort of signal. We arranged it at Christmas. Algernon is an excellent fellow, up to all the rigs. He told me if a man came and showed me his ring, I would know I could trust him. Just like the Oliphant brothers in the book Algernon started to read me during the Christmas holidays. *'Blood Brothers'* is the name of it. They weren't real brothers, only half, but they nicked their fingers with a knife and blended their blood, to become full blood brothers. Would you like to be my blood brother, Miss Stacey?" he asked hopefully.

"I'm a girl, so I couldn't be a blood brother," I demurred. "Why did Algernon take that precaution, about the ring?"

"No special reason. We were reading the book, and since we were already brothers, Algernon said we didn't have to blend our bloods, so we used the ring signal instead."

It could have been the idle amusement of a romantic college boy, or it could have been a calculated plan, as Algernon was displeased with how the Beaudels were managing his estate. At least I could not imagine any manner in which Morrison could have got the ring without the connivance of Algernon Beaudel, and that reassured me as to his good faith.

Chapter Eleven

Mrs. Beaudel did not request my presence or Lucien's at her dinner table that evening. I brought the boy down to say good-night to her, and found the saloon empty. From behind the door of her private parlor issued soft, girlish giggles, and soon the deeper tone of Wiggins, flirting his head off. There were even scuffling sounds, indicating some playful chase. I assume he caught her, no difficult chore, as there ensued a longish silence.

"Mrs. Beaudel is busy. We shan't interrupt her," I said primly to my charge.

He gave me a sage look. "We better not. She don't like to be disturbed when she is kissing Wiggins. She got very angry the last time I did it."

"That *was* naughty of you," I said, dispensing with any explanations to whitewash the trollop.

"It is naughty of her too, isn't it, Miss Stacey? It is what comes of Uncle Charles marrying a young woman. It is a May–December match, Miss Little said."

"A good lesson for you to remember," I said playfully.

"I shall get married young, and kiss my wife my own self, instead of having the butler do it. But it is very nice for Wiggins, is it not?"

"Quite an unusual perquisite to his position."

"What is a perquisite?" he asked, with an adult air.

"A little extra something besides money that goes along with a position."

"Like your being able to have meetings with Major Morrison?" he asked slyly.

"I do not consider that a perquisite by any means."

"*He* does, I think. He says you are very pretty, and wonders why you don't have a husband."

"Does he indeed!"

"He said I might just hint to discover whether you have a beau at home, if I like. Have you?"

"This is not a very subtle hint, Lucien," I said, in lieu of answering.

"What's subtle mean?" he asked.

"The lessons are over for today. It's time for bed."

"But *do* you have a beau? I told Major I would find out."

"Then you shall have to tell him you failed in your mission."

"He doesn't have a girl."

"How decent of him, since he has got a wife."

"Has he? He did not say so."

"Put on your nightshirt," I ordered, turning down his bed, to allow him some privacy.

"Would you like to read me a story?" he asked, when we were done.

"I was hoping you would ask. Get a book."

"If you like, you can read *Blood Brothers,* and learn how to become a blood sister. Algernon didn't read me the whole thing. He had to stop before he was finished, to go back to college. It has hard words, or I would have finished it myself."

This inclined me to think Algernon had used the book to pave the way for the major's coming. I wondered why he had not come sooner. *Blood Brothers* was so far from being a child's book that I had to paraphrase the whole thing, so wearing a pastime that I read him only three pages, before taking it to my room and starting at the beginning, after Lucien was tucked in. It was typical young man's fare, exciting and bloody doings, full of villains and deceit. I judged Algernon to have melodramatic tastes.

The time until eleven passed quickly. I was engrossed in Chapter Ten, waiting to find out who was the ghost, who perpetrated such ghastly doings at Widow-well Hall, the locale where the blood brothers conspired. I knew perfectly well that a headless body did not float unaided by Jeremy's window at midnight, and read on to learn who dangled the stuffed clothing from a string above. It was childish stuff, but well done enough to raise a few goose bumps. Before the major came, I decided I ought to take a peek downstairs, to ensure that Mrs. Beaudel was still entertaining her butler.

Wiggins very nearly caught me out. He was just entering the little private parlor with a fresh bottle of wine as I looked around the stairwall corner, but he was preoccupied, and did not see me. His face wore an anticipatory smile. His cravat was loose, his jacket open, his complexion flushed from whatever he was doing behind that door. The new bottle of wine indicated they were far from finished with their night's play.

I turned and darted back upstairs, down the hall to the balcony door. I had to suppress a scream to see a white face floating in the glass top of the doorway, the very part of the anatomy missing from the ghost in *Blood Brothers*. Within an instant, I realized it was Morrison, and went to admit him.

"You nearly frightened me to death," I scolded.

"Did you forget I was to come?"

"No, I just didn't expect to see you peeking in at the window. Mrs. Beaudel is belowstairs. We shan't have any interference from her."

"What is she doing with herself?"

"Nothing, she's doing it with Wiggins. Don't ask."

"That maidenly tone of disapproval makes it unnecessary to inquire. Which is Beaudel's door?" he queried, coming on tiptoes behind me down the hall.

I took him to it, tried the knob, and found it locked. "He's

110

locked Stella out of his room. The man is mad," Morrison declared.

"He's not here, remember? But it is peculiar he locked it all the same. They have adjoining rooms. Maybe we can reach his through hers. It's this one," I said, showing him. He opened it, and we went into a pretty, scented chamber, bearing all the evidence of a vain woman. There was a dresser laden with glass pots, the coverlet turned down with a lace-trimmed nightgown ready for her. Morrison's lips turned up in a lascivious smile as he glanced at it.

"Does she have a dresser?" he asked.

"Are you blind? There it is, four feet long, and covered with cosmetics."

"I refer to a woman who tends her clothing. Is some dame likely to come erupting through that other door?"

"No, one of the house servants takes care of her things."

"We'll risk it then," he said, stepping quickly and quietly across the carpeted floor, to try the adjoining door. It too was locked. "One of them has locked the other out. As his outer door is also locked, it looks as though he doesn't want her having too close a look around while he's away."

"Then he must have the Jaipur locked in his room."

"Hmm, I believe we'll go in by the hall door, just in case she and Wiggins decide to adjourn here to continue their revels."

"She wouldn't!"

"A floor can get mighty hard for what they're up to, and chairs are demmed awkward."

"There is a sofa in her parlor," I said, displaying no shock at his words, as he examined me with lively glee to watch me squirm.

He went into the hallway, took out his knife and opened the door as easily as though it were a pea pod. One flick of the knife and we were in. We had only the dim light from the hall.

"Shall I get a candle?" I asked.

"Make it snappy," he said, looking around the room, which was Spartan.

I got the candle from my own room. By the time I returned, Morrison had jimmied open the door leading to the tower.

111

"Close the hall door, just in case," he ordered. Swallowing my indignation at his abrupt manner, I did so. Together we mounted the narrow, paneled stairway to the tower room. It was octagonal in shape, the dark wooden walls swallowing up the light. It was outfitted as an office, but had no air of being much used. There was nothing on the desk but a dry ink bottle, a writing quill and dust. The room also held a small table, a cupboard and a few wooden, straight-backed chairs. All drawers in both desk and cupboard were unlocked. I need hardly say none of them contained the Jaipur. Neither did they hold anything of the least interest. Next Morrison took the taper around the room, tapping walls, then down on his hands and knees to feel for a loose floorboard.

"Do you think he has a safe or a strongbox hidden somewhere?" I asked, to have a better idea what we were searching for.

"I have no idea."

"That's helpful."

"Just look—for anything that seems out of place," he advised.

A discarded gentleman's hat, somewhat ratty in appearance, struck me as being out of place, but so obviously innocent I did not mention it. "Why did he bother to lock all those doors, if there's nothing here but dust and lumber?" Morrison asked.

"Particularly when they can be opened in the twinkling of a penknife," I added, wondering. "If you can do it, so can Mrs. Beaudel."

"He may be so naive he doesn't realize it. He *did* marry her, and that says something for his gullibility." He set the candle down and looked slowly all around the room. His eyes lit on a dark canvas, a painting of some Friday-faced gentleman in a wig and court robes. "Surely not," he said, smiling, as he stepped to the picture and lifted the frame from the wall.

Behind it was a small locked door, flush with the wall. It had a plain padlock on it, difficult enough that the penknife did not open it, but the hardware that held the padlock was screwed in. The screws could have been removed without too much effort. I waited for him to take his knife to them, but

112

he only frowned a moment, before replacing the canvas painting.

"Aren't you going to open the safe?" I asked, astonished.

"It would take too long. We know he has the place locked up. I'm willing to conclude the diamond is in here."

"After all this, you're not going to bother finishing the job?" I asked.

"I'm satisfied."

"Well *I* am not!"

"Help yourself," he said, handing me the knife, and directing a challenging smile at me.

I quickly handed it back and wiped my hands. "We can't be sure it's in there," I pointed out, hoping to talk him into finishing the job, as we had come so far.

"Sure it is. Are you—ah—coming back down with me, or do you plan to remain behind and talk to Sir Jacoby?" he enquired, with a look at the painting.

"How do you know his name?"

"With a face like that, he has to be a Jacoby," was his laconic reply. He took the candle and went to the stairs. I hurried after him. He relocked the tower door, then crossed Beaudel's room and locked the door to the hallway. "What next?" he asked, looking up and down the hallway once more. "The night is young. Care for a glass of wine?"

"You didn't bring wine with you!" I exclaimed, ready to believe it.

"I didn't think to. Charles must have some we could borrow."

"Oh no, you'd better go," I said nervously. There was not much doubt in my mind the bold man would saunter down the main staircase and take up a seat in the saloon, if given the least encouragement.

"I'll see you to your door, like a gentleman," he offered, taking hold of my elbow to walk down the hall.

"I should lock the balcony door when you leave."

"How did I come not to think of that, I wonder? It's either your big, bright eyes, or the lace confection lying on Stella's bed that has distracted me," he said, as we walked to the doorway.

Once there, he leaned comfortably against the wall and

113

blew out my candle. There was some illumination from the lamp further along the hall.

"It's not at all late. Care to come out for a drive?" he invited.

"I think you're insane."

"What are you afraid of?"

"Getting caught when I come back in."

"Good. I thought there for a minute it was the beard that was frightening you. I could shave it off if..."

"No. Really you are too ridiculous. Oh, before you go..."

"I'm not planning to leave for quite a while yet."

"Did your man get back from Tunbridge Wells?"

"Yes, he did. He discovered.... Is there nowhere we could sit down to talk? I don't mind leaning myself, but it is a hard way to treat a lady. Let's just step out and sit on the top step of the balcony, shall we? Or we could go to your room, if you prefer."

"We'll go out," I said, opening the door rather quickly, and pretending not to see his wicked smile. "What did he discover?"

"Let me put my handkerchief here, so you won't dirty your gown," he offered, unfolding a handkerchief and placing it carefully and slowly on the step.

"You are the most exasperating man! Will you tell me what you have learned?" I said, plumping down on the spread handkerchief.

"I have learned you are an ungrateful wretch. That is my last clean handkerchief. I did not have sufficient packed for the length of my visit."

"You don't need a handkerchief. You aren't suffering from a cold."

"I am not enjoying any noticeable warmth either, from your direction. The temperature is hotter belowstairs I wager. Very well then, Miss van Deusen."

"I wish you wouldn't call me that."

"What is your given name?"

"Mieke. I know it's ridiculous. My friends call me Mickey."

"That is even more ridiculous. It sounds like an Irish bruiser. Don't you have any more euphonious name I might call you?"

114

"Anna. Anna Mieke is my name."

"That is possible to utter without shuddering. Very well then, Anna, I shall tell you what was discovered. I *do* wish we had some wine. Even tea would be better than nothing."

"There is a jug of cold water on my nightstand. It will be poured over your head very soon, Major Morrison, if you don't get on with it."

"My friends call me Bertie."

I folded my arms against the chilly winds and waited. "You are feeling cold," was his next concern. "You must allow me to lend you my jacket."

"Oh, please get on with it!" I said, rather loud.

"I'm removing it as fast as I can."

"That's not what I mean."

But it felt comfortable when he placed it around my shoulders. I knew he must now be cold himself, and hoped the discomfort might hasten his story.

"Very well then, business before pleasure," he began, as he sat beside me on the hard metal steps. "Her maiden name was Stella Dumbrille. Now that is the sort of name you ought to have, Anna. I refer only to her given name, of course. It means star. Look, there is a bright, twinkling one. The north star, probably. I never did learn to tell them apart."

"What was she, before she was Mrs. Beaudel?" I got in, when he stopped for a breath.

"A milliner, from Maidstone. Alliterative, but little enough else to recommend either the occupation or the place. There wasn't time to discover her origins, but I doubt it matters. Whatever she was up to in her teens, she has doubtless outgrown. When she met Charles, she was posing as a lady of leisure at the resort at Tunbridge Wells. How does a milliner from Maidstone suddenly become a lady of leisure at the Wells, you are going to ask me. Don't despair, I am going to tell you very soon."

"Aren't you cold?" I asked, hoping to jog him along at a faster clip.

"A little," he admitted, but his solution was to move closer to me and slide his arm under his jacket, which was hung around my body. I removed it.

"Do go on. With the story, I mean," I invited.

115

"The story is the less interesting of the two diversions that are going on here, Anna," he informed me.

"That makes it very dull indeed, but do continue."

"I shall. At some point in her millinery career, she came under Wiggins's protection—actually lived in a set of rooms paid for by him. He was one of the mightier footmen working for Lord Kersey at the time. I wonder if that would be the Kersey for whom kerseymere is named? Probably not."

"We may never know that interesting point. Nor how Stella became a lady of leisure at Tunbridge Wells, at the rate we are going."

"I certainly intend to look into it. The origins of kerseymere, I mean. As to the other, I believe she fled Maidstone when he was arrested."

"At last we are getting somewhere."

"That is a matter of opinion. Wiggins was arrested for the attempted kidnapping of Kersey's son. He asked for ten thousand ransom."

"Why isn't he in jail, or hung, if they caught him?"

"They didn't exactly catch him. He was arrested on suspicion of complicity in the kidnapping. A thoroughly botched job. The boy got away, and could not positively identify Wiggins, but it seems he was off duty at the time it was done. French leave, with no intention of returning I expect. He was locked up pending the hearing, which is when Stella sat it out at Tunbridge Wells, and latched on to Beaudel. Our lenient legal system insists on guilt beyond a doubt before a man is convicted, so Wiggins squeaked off free, and followed dear Stella to Glanbury Park."

"Imagine Beaudel being fool enough to marry her. He cannot have known a thing about her."

"One assumes not. Nor about Wiggins either. I know *I* would not have my wife's lover in my employ."

"You *do* remember you have a wife, whose son died so inopportunely while you were in the Peninsula, winning the Battle of Burgos."

"Ah yes, back to Burgos. Both Wellington and I came a cropper there, did we not? Of course I have no wife. Evasions are unfortunately necessary from time to time in life."

"I have not found it to be so."

116

"Have you not, Miss van-Stacey? What a charmed life you lead, to be sure."

"Till now, I mean."

"It is *now* we are speaking of. I never found it necessary to be married before either—except once in Paris, when a certain Mademoiselle.... But you wouldn't be interested in that."

"No, I wouldn't."

"Good. It is a close-run affair I prefer to forget."

"Why don't you then? It looks as though Stella Dumbrille married old Charles thinking to get hold of the jewelry."

"And sent off to Wiggins to come along and give her a hand, and any other part of his body he wasn't using. Don't jump so, Anna. It was only his arms, and possibly lips, I was referring to. What a salacious little mind you have. There might be hope for you yet."

"You *do* think Charles is innocent then?"

"I think he is a fool. I think he spent more money than he had to bribe her with assorted luxuries, and used Lucien's money to foot the bill, probably with some weak intention of repaying it from his own estate, at some future date. But Stella is after more than bonnets and gowns. It is the Jaipur she has in mind."

"She's always urging Charles to sell the jewels. Money would be easier to spend than a large diamond. I mean, she'd have to sell it, and it could be traced back to her."

"I know what you mean. But then grabbing fifty or so thousand pounds and running also holds a hint of wrong-doing. I expect it is poor old Wiggins who will light out with the cash, and she'll join him after the talk dies down. What fools we men are for a pretty woman."

"I wonder why Beaudel went to London. He received some letter, which got him upset."

"With Algernon soon to come home and demand an accounting, and with five thousand pounds to be explained away, he may be trying to raise the wind. If so, it is an auspicious time to make my reasonably generous offer for the Jaipur. He might think he can get away with shaving five thousand from the price, if it's high enough."

117

"You'll have to make sure Stella doesn't manage to steal the money. Otherwise, you are playing right into her hands."

"That *did* occur to me, Anna. I am not quite so besotted with the moonlight that I overlooked that difficulty."

"What will you do? How will you arrange it?"

"In some fiendishly clever manner."

"I expect you'll need my help."

"Thank you for the offer."

"Glad to be of service. Now that your man is back from Tunbridge Wells, will you set him to discover where Mr. Kirby is?"

"I too am happy to be of service. Why is it, do you suppose, *my* services are so much more onerous than your own?"

"It won't put *you* out much to send a man to London."

"It will put me out several pounds. It will also put me out of the services of my valet. No clean handkerchiefs in the foreseeable future. Do you sew at all?"

"Not if I can help it, but this one is hardly used," I said, arising to hand him the rag I sat on.

He shook it out, disbursing a fine powder of dust from the step. "Not more than a cup of soot in it. It will be good for another week. Is it good-night then, my dear?"

"*Au revoir*, Major Morrison."

"We were going to forget that unfortunate Parisian episode."

"I wasn't reminding you of it, only of our meeting tomorrow. *Au revoir* means till we meet again."

"I can hardly wait."

"You will be in the meadow? I want to keep informed of what is happening."

"Do the swallows forget to return to Dover in the spring?" he asked, smiling lazily.

"No, we have the dirtiest rocks in England to prove they are there."

"May I have my coat, please? The air is getting chillier. I can't think what accounts for it. I have exerted every effort to be civil."

I handed it to him. "Would you mind holding it for me? It fits so closely it requires two of us to get it on. Weston is to blame. The result is impressive though, is it not?" he asked,

118

easing his arms into it and smoothing it over his chest, where it did indeed look impressive.

"Speechless, I see," he ran on, when I made no reply. "I had not thought it quite that impressive. Modesty was ever my failing. What's yours? Other than that sad tendency to muteness, and a little lack of levity."

"I believe it must be blindness, Major. I see nothing impressive in a jacket that does not quite fit properly across the shoulders."

He laughed good-humoredly. "I misjudged you, to accuse you of a lack of humor. I wonder if my reading of your character in other respects has been equally deficient. Shall we test it?"

"In what manner?"

"Like this," he said, swooping me into his arms.

It felt very strange, having a wiry brush of beard and moustache tickling my face. Other than that, it was rather cozy, being encircled in his warm arms, there in the cool night air. I did not push him away, or feel much frightened, nor did I encourage him to continue by returning any pressure of his lips. After a moment, he released me.

"What is the verdict? Was your reading of me deficient, like so many other things you do?"

"Inconclusive. I hold the beard to blame."

"By all means let us blame the beard, and not the wearer. Good-night."

I opened the door and went in, locking it behind me. His white face with black chin was still there at the glass door top staring at me. Any reading of his expression was difficult with half his face covered. Perhaps he was not smiling at all, as I thought. He blew me a kiss, cocked his curled beaver over his eye, gave a salute, and left.

It was not until I got into bed and reviewed our talk that one rather important fact occurred to me. If he were to actually *buy* the Jaipur, he must be a very wealthy man. He had mentioned a fiendishly clever plan, but it would have to be very clever indeed to make the banks honor such a large check, if he hadn't the money.

Chapter Twelve

Mr. Beaudel came back the next day shortly after lunch. Wiggins returned to being a punctilious butler; Mrs. Beaudel to being a dissatisfied young wife; and I to being a governess. Beaudel spent the afternoon in his office. Just as I picked up my pelisse to go to the meadow with Lucien, Mrs. Beaudel stuck her head into my room. "Could I borrow you for a moment, Miss Stacey?" she asked. She looked excited. Her eyes were sparkling, and her color high.

"Certainly," I replied.

"Come along to my room," she ordered. I followed her down the hallway, curious.

"I am just finishing up a note to be delivered, and as you and Lucien are going out, you can deliver it for me." She sat at her desk to seal up her letter, while my heart sank in dismay. I looked around the chamber while she was busy. It was tidy. I noticed nothing amiss until I happened to look at an upholstered chair in the corner. She had a silken scarf laid out on it, with a small pile of clean linens on top, and a toothbrush. Were it not for the toothbrush, I would hardly have glanced at it. It was not enough clothing to suggest a trip—no gowns, no shoes, no trunk or bag for that matter. Unless she meant to roll those few linens up in a scarf like an itinerant worker, she was not preparing for flight.

"Where did you want us to take the note?" I asked, hoping it was to a close neighbor.

"Into the village."

"I was going to take Lucien to the meadow, for his daily ride," I ventured.

"If you are like Miss Little, you would prefer to do your walking in the village to anywhere else. Take the carriage if you prefer, and have your walk after you get there."

I didn't say anything, but she saw the dismay in my face. "I'll give you a little pourboire, to make it worth your while," she added. "Just drop this note off at the milliner's shop for me. The new one at the edge of town, Mrs. Cantor—not the old-fashioned shop across from the inn. I swear they have nothing but round bonnets. You don't have to wait for a reply. Just hand it to the housekeeper. I want the feathers on my new bonnet changed to white." She lifted the sealed note from the desk, rooted a shilling from a porcelain tray holding loose change, and handed them both to me. "You won't forget."

"No, I won't. Thank you," I said, accepting both, as I was not ingenious enough to think of a reason for refusing.

Back in my room, my next thought was to get a message to Major Morrison, but there was no one in the house I knew well enough to ask. I would have to stand him up. My second thought was to try to discover what was in the note. Such was my distrust of Madam that even a note to her milliner fell under suspicion.

The single sheet was sealed with a plain wafer, but by compressing the folded end, it was possible to peer in and see part of the message. There was no mention of bonnets or feathers in the bit I could see, nor was the message long enough that this might have been included in another passage. The few words visible from the sides were "hire the place," "name of Mr. Wel..." and "Wiggins will." The remainder of the message could not be seen, but her signature

121

at the bottom was "Stella"—not Mrs. Beaudel, as one would expect in a note to one's milliner.

Lucien came to the door, impatient to be off. He was not troubled to have the outing changed. He was bubbling with different news.

"Major Morrison is coming this afternoon. I hope we are back in time to see him," he told me. "Uncle Charles said he is coming to see the rose Jaipur. If he likes it, he will buy it from me. I will be a wealthy young man," he added, obviously quoting his uncle.

I was stunned with the speed of Morrison's offer. "What time is he coming?" I asked, wondering if he had planned to stand me up in the meadow, and I worrying about doing the same to him.

"At four o'clock. We can be back, if we hurry."

There was no dallying after hearing this. I threw my bonnet on my head and hastened to the stairs. I was not the only one in a hurry. Mrs. Beaudel had the carriage harnessed and waiting for us. Mrs. Cantor's millinery shop was not so much a shop as a cottage with a discreet hand-painted cardboard sign in the window. There was no excess of traffic. In fact, there was none at all except ourselves. A young female servant in a mobcap answered the door. Her mistress was two steps behind her. She was a big-boned dame in her forties, with black hair that ill-suited her pale face. She wore a decent dark gown, but managed to look like a trollop despite it.

"What do you want?" she asked me, in a very common accent.

One would think a milliner would assume I wanted a bonnet, but this did not seem to occur to her. The servant handed her the note, which she grabbed anxiously, then she slammed the door in my face. The trip was accomplished so quickly that I took Lucien to the meadow after we returned, in case the major should be so patient as to wait until three o'clock.

From across the meadow I saw him, sitting on a rock with his chin in his hands, like Patience on a monument. "You had better have a very good excuse!" was his opening salvo.

"We have been to the village."

"Not good enough," he said, arising to look belligerently down his nose at us.

122

I explained how it had come about, as Lucien rode his pony in large circles around us, looking to see that we admired his seat.

"Does she know I am coming to look at the diamond this afternoon?" he asked.

"I imagine so. Beaudel told Lucien, so it is no secret."

"Let us assume she does, and be prepared for the worst."

"She won't just steal the diamond at gunpoint. She could have had it any time, if it is in the safe as we think. You should have checked, to be certain."

"Is it possible she's stupid enough to think I'll pay cash? They've hired a place; she has clothes packed—isn't that what you said? She and Wiggins plan to grab the money and run."

"Not *many* clothes. Just a few linens and a toothbrush."

"She could hardly load a carriage down with trunks. If she knows I'm coming at four, she may plan to steal the money tonight, before he gets it into a bank. She'd count on his infatuation with her to delay his calling in the authorities, I expect."

"You'll be paying by cheque?"

"Yes."

"Do you have enough money—fifty thousand pounds, is it?"

"The sum is not settled until I examine the gem. As to the money, yes, I can afford it. That sets you to wondering, I see."

"They won't trust a stranger's cheque for such a sum."

"I am not a stranger, but a good friend of Sacheverel. Furthermore, I took the precaution of getting a cheque certified for fifty thousand. If any little extra is required to close the deal, that could be uncertified."

"It's hard to believe they count on your paying cash. And where does Mrs. Cantor come into it?"

"Mrs. Beaudel was a milliner herself, before coming here. It might be an old colleague. I shall discover whether the woman is a new addition to the village. Or you could do that, from the girls at the Park."

"I wonder if they worked together before, on that kidnapping of Kersey's son."

"Very likely. There was some older couple in on it. It was

they who had arranged to hire a place...." He stopped at that telling phrase, to tug at his beard. "Kidnapping!" he exclaimed.

"Precisely my own thought!"

"Criminals *will* stick with the same sort of crime, same method of executing it, and so on."

"That's true. I've often heard my father say so, when discussing jewel robberies. They're going to kidnap Lucien. Oh, my God, Major, we have to let Beaudel know."

"Just a minute," he said, holding up his hands. "They're not going to do anything till Beaudel has my money. Yes, this is more sensible. Beaudel banks the money, and then has to get cash to pay them off to get Lucien back. Did Lucien see Mrs. Cantor?"

"Yes, he came with me to her shop."

"And Stella *knew* he was going with you, so she didn't care if he saw the woman. That's odd. I mean, you'd think she would use someone unknown to him. Unless they plan to *kill* the boy..."

"Surely not!"

"They're really getting in deep if that's the plan. But how can they let him go home, if he can identify her? I'm assuming, of course, that neither Stella nor Wiggins take an active part in the kidnapping, but only engineer it."

"There must be more people involved."

"There are already four. They wouldn't want to split it up any more than necessary. The neater plan would be for Stella and Wiggins to sit tight at the Park till the money was handed over, then after a few months, she could have a riproaring fight with Beaudel and leave without attaching any suspicion she was involved in the kidnapping. And she wouldn't have any reason to have her linens and toothbrush packed up for that course, would she?"

"No. Bad as she is, I'm sure she wouldn't plan to *murder* Lucien. She rather likes him. She's greedy, but she's not *vicious*," I said, always harking back in my mind to this dreadful possibility. "Maybe they're not planning to kidnap him at all. We have no reason to suppose it's to be a kidnapping."

"They kidnapped before. That's their racket. Maybe they

don't plan to kidnap *Lucien*. Maybe it's old Beaudel.... No, he has to be home to arrange the funds. Who else is there? Who would Beaudel fork over fifty thousand for? There's only his nephew and—his wife." he finished, with a curious little smile.

"What—Stella kidnaps herself?" I asked, with an incredulous laugh.

"Why not?" he asked reasonably. "She wouldn't meet much resistance, would she? You may be sure after she was let free, she would not put the finger on the Cantors. It would be some Frenchmen or Irishmen who did it. The remainder of the plan still holds. She goes home for a reasonable time, then has her falling out with Charles and goes to join the conspirators. The four of them are off and running—anywhere they choose. It would be logical for Wiggins to leave at the same time. *She* hired him. He might even be the reason for the fight with Charles, to give him an unexceptionable excuse to resign his position. I think that covers all bases. A pretty clever scheme."

I went over it mentally for loopholes, and found none. In fact, I liked the scheme, as it left out all danger of a physical sort to Lucien. Only his fortune was at jeopardy. "So what should we do?" was my next question.

"An ounce of prevention. You'll see."

"Please tell me. I'm dying to know."

"There isn't time. I have the details to work out. I have to nip into the village and have a word with the expert who is going to authenticate the Jaipur for me. Mills is his name."

"Albert Mills? I know him, and he knows *me*. I must stay out of sight."

"I'll tip him the clue he's never seen you before."

"When did you arrange for him to come?" I asked, trailing after him as he hastened toward his mount, tethered near the stream.

"My man followed Beaudel to London. He toured the jewel merchants, inquiring about possible markets and price for the Jaipur, indicating it was for sale. My man had instructions to ask Mills to come, if that was Beaudel's errand. Love and Wirgmans indicated to him that fifty thousand was a fair price, so that will be my offer. I think he'd take it. A bird

125

in the hand. He'll want the money before Algernon comes home, asking questions. He'll tell him he took forty-five, which is not a *bad* price, not low enough to cause instant suspicion."

"I don't suppose your man had time to enquire after Mr. Kirby, in London?" I remembered to ask.

"As a matter of fact, he did," he answered, which surprised me. "I have a note of his address here. He lives nearby, in a cottage about five miles from the town. Here, I'll jot down the direction."

He scribbled them out very quickly and handed them to me.

"Oh, thank you. I'll write him this very day. Because you know, if we aren't going to prove Stella stole those diamonds, it doesn't do Papa any good at all. He is still languishing in that prison."

"Yes, but I sent him a bottle of the very best brandy, and all the latest papers. Later I shall take Mills around to see him. That will prove a pleasant diversion, to have an old colleague to talk to."

"It will break his heart that he isn't to get to see the Jaipur."

"I may be able to arrange that too," he said, and laughed, a reckless, excited laugh.

I mistrusted the mood he was in. Amidst all the confusion of stealing and kidnapping and hiring a place by the Cantors, we had lost track of freeing Papa. It was clearly not a top priority of the major's, but how had *I* allowed myself to be led so far astray?

"What is the matter, Anna?" he asked suddenly. Glancing up from my fit of distraction, I saw he regarded me with troubled, gentle eyes, and felt guilty at my ill thoughts of him.

"I'm worried about my father, of course."

"Don't. He'll be free very soon. That's a promise."

I felt an instinctive urge to trust him, when he looked at me in that way. "Should you prevent the kidnapping? Wouldn't it be better to let them go ahead with it, catch them in the act, I mean? How else can we prove anything?"

"Trust me."

"Couldn't I help in some way? I'll be there, in the house. I can spy, see if she leaves. There ought to be someone set to watch the Cantors too, and—oh, any number of things," I said, as he impatiently mounted his gelding, wanting to leave. "We need a whole army."

"You don't need anyone but me. I will handle it," he insisted. "There is no counting on any of them to behave as ladies and gentlemen, my dear. They might take it very much amiss if they found you lurking at keyholes, or in the back of carriages. God only knows what shocking things your beautiful eyes would be exposed to. We don't want you quite disenchanted with relations between the sexes. You're timid enough already. Or was it the beard?" he asked, bending down and taking my hands in his.

I looked around the meadow for Lucien. He was dismounting to try for tadpoles in the stream. "I have to go immediately," Morrison said. "See you at eleven at our trysting place, as usual? The highlight of my day."

"All right."

"If for any reason I can't make it, don't worry. I'll be in touch somehow." He released my hands to take up the reins, then kissed his finger and leaned down to place it on my lips. "Till I get around to removing the whiskers, we must use a go-between. Very unsatisfactory," he added, with a long look at my lips. I felt the same way.

I called Lucien. Morrison waved to us both and galloped off towards the village.

"I expect he is going to get the money to buy my diamond," Lucien said, looking after him. "I will give you a present when I get it, Miss Stacey."

"You will do nothing of the sort, sir. It is not the thing to be buying presents for ladies you hardly know."

"I know you well. I like you too. I will give you a new book to read me."

"Ah well, if *that* is the sort of valuable gift you have in mind, I accept."

"You can keep it after we are done with it," he offered handsomely.

"Lovely."

"And if it is good, I can borrow it back when I want to look

127

at the pictures again," he added, rather regretting his generosity already. He remounted his pony, and we went home.

Wiggins was in the kitchen when we entered by the back door. I could hardly hide my feelings for the miserable wretch, and to make it worse, he chose that day to flirt with me, while Tess looked on, with laughter in her eyes.

"Your playing hard to get is paying off," she told me, after he returned abovestairs. "Why you'll be making the madam jealous, the way he's throwing his hanky at you. What did he mean about spending your shilling?" she asked.

"Madam gave me a shilling for delivering a note for her," I replied, noticing that Wiggins was very well aware of my trip.

"She's generous! She never gives *me* that much. Where did you have to go?"

"To the milliner. Has Mrs. Cantor been here for long?"

"Who's Mrs. Cantor?" she asked. "I never heard of her."

"The milliner in the village—the one at the edge of town."

"Everybody goes to Mrs. Blossom. She makes the best bonnets hereabouts. Madam gets all hers there. Has she found someone new to patronize?"

"It looks that way," I replied, but I knew the patronizing had nothing to do with bonnets.

Chapter Thirteen

I am not superstitious, but it is curious all the same that
Chapter Thirteen should contain such a piece of bad luck.
After we returned from our walk, Mr. Beaudel asked us to
step into his office.

"Has the lad been telling you we have a possible purchaser
coming to look at the Jaipur diamond?" he asked me. He had
changed into a new jacket and clean shirt for the grand occasion.

"He mentioned it to me," I replied.

"Major Morrison is the chap who wants it. The fellow who
bought the Italian necklace, you know. I don't know what is
best to be done, but it would be a wonderful relief not to have
the worry of such a valuable thing in the house, just waiting
to be stolen, and the bank vaults not a whole lot safer either.
I wonder that a fellow like Morrison, with so much of the
ready in his pocket, ever bothered his head with soldiering,
but I could not like to quiz him about it. Sacheverel's word

must be good enough for *me* that he has the money, and came by it honestly. We'll let him worry about keeping the gem safe, if he gives us a firm offer, that is to say."

I wondered if he had been so concerned for its safety before his marriage. Next Beaudel turned his attention to his nephew.

"You will want to be there for the transaction. It is your property, Lucien; you must be there. And if you don't want to sell, just say so. I am only your guardian. You will want to put a clean suit on him, Miss Stacey. A fellow doesn't do such big business as this every day of his life. You bring him down. You might be curious to see the fabulous jewel yourself, before it leaves the house."

"I would love to see it," I admitted, a trifle too eagerly, but he did not notice my enthusiasm. He was smiling at Lucien. He seemed such a nice, kindly old man, I was sorry to have to expose him.

"I will come down to say good-bye to it," Lucien declared, then took my hand to pull me upstairs for the toilette.

"Why didn't Major Morrison come home with us?" he asked, a logical question, requiring a logical answer.

"He had to go into town to pick up the expert who is going to look at the gem with him. Mills is his name."

"The first man who came to be an expert stole some diamonds. Aunt Stella told me so."

"Did she? When was that, Lucien?"

"Just before you came here."

"When did she tell you, I mean? When were you speaking to her alone?"

"Last night after supper. She came upstairs to put on a new gown, and I asked her why, when Uncle Charles was away. She was putting it on to please Wiggins, but she didn't say so. She said it was for me, and let me choose it."

"What one did you choose?" I asked, concealing my smile at his knowing mind.

"I chose the blue. Wiggins likes it best. I heard him tell her once she looked like a cloud in it, floating across the lawn."

"He is very romantic."

"Why don't you like him then?"

"He's all right, just not my type."

"That's what I thought. I told Major Morrison you didn't like Wiggins, when he asked me if you ever had private talks with him, like Aunt Stella does. He meant making love."

"He asked you that?" I demanded.

"A long time ago, the day you made us take you to the village. I think he didn't like you so much then, but he does now. He didn't ask me about your beau today. I'm glad, because I still have failed in my mission," he reminded me, hinting for an answer.

"You can tell Major Morrison I *do* have a beau, back home in Norfolk. A very steady beau, whom I shall be marrying as soon as I get back."

"You are not leaving so soon!" he exclaimed, causing me to realize I had blundered, in my vexation with the talkative, nosy major.

"Of course not. *When* I leave, is all I meant," I explained, but it was a cruel trick to play an innocent child. He just became fond of one governess after another, and she left. This reminded me of Miss Little, whose vanishing was still unexplained.

"Can I wear my Sunday jacket with the velvet lapels?" he asked, going to the clothespress.

"Why not?" I humored him in this conceit. He looked every inch the little gentleman when his hair was brushed into place. Uncertain what degree of elegance was expected of me, I did no more than brush my hair and put on a gold chain with a small pearl suspended from it. All attention would be on the rose diamond.

We waited until five past four, to see if we were sent for, but as we were not, I took Lucien down to his uncle's office. Major Morrison was just being shown in, with Mr. Mills, a cadaverous, pale man of sixty-odd years in his wake. Not so much as a blink betrayed our former acquaintance, when Beaudel made his introductions. Morrison too treated me like a mere acquaintance, making me aware what a good actor he was.

As Mr. Beaudel drew a leather pouch out of his desk, I risked casting one frightened eye on Morrison. He raised his brows silently and smiled, enjoying the charade. Soon everything else was forgotten. The rose Jaipur sat in the palm of Beaudel's hand, a magnificent rose diamond pear, as large as a small chestnut. At four o'clock, the light was not as bright as it could be, but the gem caught the weak sunlight and shot it back in a million prisms. Its clarity was so great, and its cut so exact, it was the most exquisite jewel I had ever seen. Low gasps were emitted on all sides. I felt a stab of regret that my father could not be present. Even a jewel merchant had few opportunities to view such a spectacular stone as this.

Beaudel took it up between his thumb and forefinger. "They tell me the thing is twenty-five carats. It strikes me it is too large to be worn in any other way than hanging as a pendant. I expect that is how you will have it set, Major, if you buy?" As he spoke, he offered it to the major. He took it to the window, turning it this way and that.

"Yes, that was my plan," he said, frowning and looking at it.

"Is there something the matter?" Beaudel asked.

It was at that moment that I noticed Mrs. Beaudel was not present, which was odd, as she had been on the other occasions.

"You take a look at it, Mills," Morrison said, handing it to him.

Mr. Mills took it, hefted it in his palm, then held it to the window. "Can't be sure. She feels right," he said, pulling his loupe from his pocket, to be stuck into his eye. There with the sunlight falling on the diamond, he examined it carefully for perhaps a minute, which seemed endless. "The best-cut piece of glass I have ever seen. Definitely paste though," he said, handing it back to Beaudel.

The man turned ashen. He made a strange sound in his throat, and clutched at his heart. I was sure he was going to fall down dead of a heart attack on the very spot. We all stared at him until some trace of color returned to his cheeks.

"That's what I thought," Morrison said blandly, lifting the thing from Mills' fingers.

"Strass, certainly," Mills spoke on, in the voice of authority. Just so had I heard my father speak to his clients, as though lecturing them. "A fine piece of work. I wouldn't be surprised if old Josef Strass himself hadn't manufactured this piece. He has an ingenious system—a melt of quartz, with lead oxide and some potassium carbonate. What was used to achieve this wonderful rose hue, I wonder? Some oxide of copper, I expect. What do you think, Major?"

"Some mixture of copper and iron, perhaps," Morrison said, discussing it as objectively as though fifty thousand pounds had not just flown out the window.

"I still like it. I shall keep it, if you don't want it," Lucien told them, and was allowed, as the thing was only glass, to hold it in his own hands and peer at the light through it. After his examination, he handed it to me. I had been figuring how I might get my hands on the fabulous rock, for whatever else it was, it was still very beautiful and interesting. It was hard to credit it was not a diamond. Hefting it, looking at it with the naked eye, did not convince me it was not a diamond either. The weight felt right.

"Are you sure, Mr. Mills?" I asked.

"Positive, Miss Stacey," he replied, using my assumed name as though he had never known me by any other. I looked at the loupe he held, wishing I might see the gem through it, to determine he spoke the truth, but I could not very well ask for it, when I was posing as an ignorant governess.

Mr. Beaudel stood stricken dumb with shock throughout it all. Whoever had switched the stone, I was morally certain he was not the culprit. It was impossible not to feel sorry for him. "I don't understand. I don't see how it could have happened," he gasped at last.

"When is the last time you were certain of the gem's authenticity? When was it last examined, I mean?" Mills enquired politely.

"It hasn't been looked at by an expert for three years—three years ago in London it was studied by a potential buyer, but we didn't care for the price he offered. If only we had taken forty thousand! It hasn't left the house since that time. I have kept it under lock and key. It can't be a fake. Look again," he pleaded.

Both Mills and Morrison were happy to oblige him, and to confirm their mutual conviction that it was Strass glass.

"A very fine piece of work," Mills kept insisting, as though that were any consolation, when he went on to confirm it was undoubtedly glass, and not diamond.

It was Morrison who diverted the talk to wonder whether the switch could not have taken place in London three years ago.

"Impossible. It was never out of my hands. I *slept* with it in my fingers, and a pistol under my pillow," Beaudel assured him. He had sunk on to a chair, his head in his hands, actually moaning. I looked from him to the two men. There was no mercy in their faces. They were perfectly satisfied to have shattered his life. And then I happened to think again of Stella. Now I knew why she was not here, intruding her presence. She had done it, switched stones, any time over the months she had been here, with easy access to it, hidden away in that toy safe I could have opened myself with a screw driver.

"Of course if you are not satisfied, you can have someone else look at it for you," Mills said offhandedly.

"Yes! Yes, that will be best," Beaudel said, lifting his head, to stare at us, distracted with grief and worry, but with now a tiny light of hope.

"I understand Dutch van Deusen is right here, in town," Morrison mentioned.

"Excellent! You couldn't do better," Mills seconded him.

"No!" I exclaimed. It was pure, undiluted instinct. A moment earlier I had wished my father could be here, but I didn't want him involved now. He had been duped once in this house. To be put in a position where he might conceivably be held accountable for this monstrous crime was infinitely worse. Everyone looked at me, startled at my vehemence, when by rights I should not have spoken at all. "He—he is the man who—who stole your stones the other time," I said to Beaudel.

"I wouldn't let the man darken my door," Beaudel said flatly.

"Rubbish. Dutch van Deusen no more took your diamonds than I did," Mills stated. "He is as honest as the day is long. There is something very havey-cavey going on here, Mr. Beaudel. *I* don't know what it is, but I would suggest you look

134

into your—staff very closely." The word "staff" was hesitated over enough to give the idea it was not his first choice of word, or his true meaning. Or so it seemed to me.

"He *does* know gems, whatever else might be said of the man," Morrison tossed in.

"Knows more about them than I do myself, and I wouldn't say that of more than two or three men in the kingdom," Mills added.

Beaudel looked bewildered, but in the end, I believe he hoped van Deusen might prove the others wrong. "We'll have him come," he decided. "I won't let the diamond go to him, but he can come here, providing the constable is with him, and stays with him while he makes his examination."

"Good enough," Morrison agreed at once, with an air of satisfaction.

Questions teamed through my poor head. I wanted to warn Morrison that Stella might even at that moment be making off with the real stone. I looked a worried message to him. He smiled blandly and turned to Beaudel.

"How shall we arrange it? It might be best if I go into the town and bring him back, with a constable, of course."

"Yes, go ahead. Will you stay, Mr. Mills?"

Again I shot a pleading look to the major. "I shall be back as soon as possible," he said, and bowed his way out the door. I ran out after him, hoping for a private word, but already Wiggins was handing him his hat and cane, holding the door for him.

"Is there something wrong, Miss?" Wiggins asked politely.

I stared at him, trying to read on that handsome face whether he was being boldly satirical, whether he knew perfectly well what was wrong, and was laughing up his sleeve at us all.

"No, nothing," I said, and turned to Lucien, who had trailed out at my heels.

Beaudel called Wiggins to the office. I heard him tell the butler to call Mrs. Beaudel down. Instead of going back upstairs with my charge, I said to him, "We shall wait here quietly in the saloon, till Major Morrison comes back."

"Good. I would like to see the constable. I wonder if he will bring his gun."

135

He opened up one of Stella's fashion magazines and perused it as happily as though it were a children's book, while I sat thinking. I heard Stella's soft footfalls hastening toward the office. The door was closed behind her. In about four minutes, she came out. Wiggins must have been loitering close by, though I did not see him.

"What's up?" he asked in a loud whisper, not realizing we were in the saloon.

"The diamond is a fake. It's only glass," she said, her voice high with incredulity. "And I know he thinks *I* took it. I could see it in his eyes, though he didn't suggest it in front of the other man."

"The devil you say! Who says it is a fake?" Wiggins answered, his tone throbbing with excitement.

"That expert in there, come down from London. How is it *possible?* Stanley, you didn't..."

"No, *I* didn't, my darling, dashing Stella. If you think you can fleece me..."

The door opened suddenly behind them, and Beaudel's voice was heard. "Will you please order some tea for us, Stella," he asked.

"Of course, my dear," she said sweetly. "You must not distress yourself. It will be all a mistake. You'll see." Beaudel went back in the office and closed the door.

"What do we do now?" Wiggins asked her.

"We order tea, Wiggins, and make it snappy. We have to keep the old fool in good humor, don't we? This is no time for him to turn on me. That wouldn't do at all."

"But if the diamond is gone..."

"We don't know for sure. Get it, I say!" She spoke angrily, then turned and fled up the stairs. I took her words for confirmation she was to be kidnapped, and Beaudel to ransom her with Lucien's money.

When silence returned outside, I went on with my thinking and figuring. Stella and Wiggins hadn't stolen the diamond. And if not they, then who? Who else knew where it was but the major, myself, and Beaudel? Beaudel was as innocent as I in the affair. His ashen face left no doubt about it. And that left only Major Morrison, who was now on his way to bring my father, to be involved again at the scene of the crime.

Lucien went on quietly turning pages, smiling at the pretty pictures of fashionable ladies. I was grateful, as it left me free to try to make sense of this latest turn. My main concern was for Papa. I didn't see how this could make his situation worse than before. He was coming to examine a stone already declared fake, so they could not blame him. But it really had not looked like glass. It looked amazingly like a beautiful, big, brilliant diamond. Mills would certainly know, however. I tried thinking in different directions.

Was it a ploy on Morrison's part to make him drop the charge against Papa? If he came and said the diamond was indeed a diamond, and Mills was talked into agreeing, would Beaudel be so grateful he would let my father go Scot free? I wondered too if Morrison had possibly corrupted Mills, had him call a diamond Strass glass. But again it made no sense. If the diamond were a diamond, my father would say so.

I had made no advance, but was only more confused, when my father was shown in, about an hour later. Morrison and the constable were with him—so degrading to have to have that constable along. I hurried into the hallway, anxious for a look at him. He was not the haggard, worn man I expected to see, after his incarceration. He looked well, clean-shaven, cheeks not sunken from starvation, shirt not filthy. Really he appeared just fine, which was a great relief to me. Only his eyes betrayed we two were anything more than strangers. They lingered on me for a long minute, then he went into the office. I followed them in, with Lucien. We had not been asked, but everyone was so upset, we got in without being told to leave.

Mills was holding the alleged Jaipur when Papa entered. He handed it to him. My father followed Mills's procedure of hefting the stone, examining it by the window and so on. Like Mills, he turned sadly to Beaudel to declare the thing a fake. I had to accept it then, and hard on the heels of my acceptance came the cold, certain knowledge that it was Major Morrison and no one else who had stolen the original. And I who had led him to it, opened the door for him, held a candle while he found the secret spot behind the portrait in the tower room. I even knew why he had not wanted to open the door, to see the diamond. He had been afraid I would know the stone was genuine, when he hoped to make folks believe the substitution had taken place much earlier. It was Morrison who deserved the constable at his elbow. He should be in the roundhouse, and not my innocent father. And I should too, for being an accessory to theft.

Chapter Fourteen

Mills, my father and Major Morrison discussed the matter for some minutes with Beaudel, enquiring whether he would call in the Bow Street Runners and so on, but no decision was come to before the men left. Lucien listened with interest, not as downcast as he would have been had he realized his position.

"We should let Algernon know," he told Beaudel.

"I will take care of it, child."

"You haven't taken very good care of my diamond. I will do it myself," he replied, not in a bold way, but matter-of-factly. The old man was close to tears, or perhaps beyond them. He had aged a decade that afternoon.

"I will try to undo the damage," Beaudel promised, his shoulders squaring, a firmer look taking possession of his countenance. He pulled the draw cord and requested Wiggins to send Mrs. Beaudel to his office. I took Lucien upstairs.

It seemed Beaudel had finally admitted to himself that his

wife was an adventuress. He could hardly be unaware of her carrying on in an unwifely manner. She took but slim pains to hide it from him. Ironically, when he was about to confront her with her treachery, he chose an act of which she was innocent. I knew I should be active, doing something to bring Morrison to justice, but sat on like a statue, thinking, thinking, thinking.

My every train of thought led to the same conclusion. Morrison had stolen the Jaipur, at some time after I had shown him its hiding place. Why he had decided to draw attention to its theft by offering to purchase it was a mystery. His escape would have been easier had he just left the neighborhood quietly. So he *wanted* everyone to know it had been stolen, as long as no suspicion was directed toward himself. Beaudel suspected his wife, and for that reason hesitated to call in the law. And if the law was not to be called in, Morrison would get away clean, without so much as a question being asked of him. The only person who could point a finger at him was myself, the daughter of an incarcerated felon, who had lied to get herself into the house. To put an extra knot in the ties binding my hands, Morrison had contrived to have my father dragged into it. Already suspect, it would be natural to assume Papa and I had connived together in the theft.

I longed to talk to my father, but to go to jail was tantamount to announcing my close connection to him. I was not clever enough to invent any logical excuse to call on an accused man. I had fallen neatly into Morrison's trap, baited with his chivalrous flirting, his repeated promises of helping my father, his injunctions to trust him. It must have been laughably easy for him to wind me round his finger, an inexperienced fool like me, who had never had a beau in her life.

Tess brought our dinner up on two trays while I still sat pondering. Lucien attacked his with his customary relish, but I did not even go to the table. I paced the room, trying to find some solution, some way to trap the major, without putting my father in worse jeopardy.

I stuffed my hands in my pockets as I walked, mindlessly fingering a bit of paper that had somehow got there. I pulled it out, and found myself staring at the directions to reach Mr.

Kirby, only five miles from Chelmsford. I had forgotten, in the throes of other matters, that Morrison had given it to me that afternoon. Morrison—was there any trusting him, even in this detail? Might it not be a trick, a trap? With all other options closed to me, I decided I must give it a try. Whoever Mr. Kirby was, he was rich, and thus with some influence. He knew something was peculiar, here at Glanbury Park. He had hinted as much to Papa before we left London. He might even know Morrison was a scoundrel—that might have been the meaning of his hint. It was imperative that I see him.

Getting away would be difficult, but with the house in an uproar over the theft, it would not be impossible. I did not ask Beaudel's permission to go. When I got to his office door, I heard him ringing a peal over Stella, who replied in tones of outraged virtue that she didn't know what he was talking about. I continued down to the kitchen and told Cook I had to make a quick visit into town.

"If it's for cloves for your toothache, Miss Stacey, I have some in my room," she offered, not suspecting any trickery from me.

"No, it's not that," I said vaguely. "I just wanted to ask if you or Tess would watch Lucien for a while. I am taking the gig."

"Fine, my dear. Do you want a boy to go with you? It will be dark before you're back."

"No, thanks. I'll hurry."

I left no message with the Beaudels, in case they should inquire for me. I didn't think they would. They had enough problems to make them forget an inconsequential governess.

It was dusk when I set out in the slow gig for Kirby's home. My route took me two miles along the major road toward Chelmsford, until I reached a side road called Mc-Master's Lane. There was nothing frightening while I stayed on the main road. Traffic was moderate, and the sun still visible on the horizon. It was about five minutes down McMaster's Lane that it finally set, casting me into heavy shadows, as I trekked alone into the darkness. I had not even brought a lantern. Before long, it was pitch black. Bushes encroached on the narrow path; from time to time, a soft, leafed branch would brush my cheek, sending my heart leap-

141

ing into my throat. Sounds of the country night were all around me, alien to my city ears, but holding great menace.

I very nearly lost courage and stopped at the first farmhouse that showed a light. I had to take myself by the scruff of the neck and remind myself what was at stake. I fought down the betraying notion that I could go home and return tomorrow by daylight. Tomorrow might be too late. Morrison might be on his way to Paris or London or Rome by then, with his ill-gotten gains.

About a mile down the road, the few farmhouses previously encountered petered out. Utter darkness lay beyond. There was considerable doubt in my mind that Mr. Kirby had a residence here at all. I had only the major's word for it. And even if I *did* find Kirby, who was to say he would help? He had proved so elusive throughout the whole ordeal, I was ready at times to wonder if he even existed. But he *did* exist, of course. It was he who had catapulted my father and me into this mess. Yes, of course he existed. He was interested in the Jaipur, and he would help me to recover it and rescue Papa. It was only these reassurances that gave me the courage to jog on, down the black lane.

It was difficult to gauge distances in the slow-moving vehicle. On foot, I can judge a mile pretty accurately. In a regular carriage by daylight too one gets some idea of the ground covered, the number of blocks and so on. But in the dark, seeing nothing but your hands a light blur in front of you, and occasionally a flickering shadow that must be the horse's tail, you lose all track of the distance traversed. It could have been a mile or a hundred miles I had gone, when at last I saw a white cottage nestled off to the left, with cosy lights twinkling. As I went closer, I saw it was stucco, as the Major had said, with a rounded archway over the front door. I was so very happy to have reached my destination it did not occur to me to wonder why a man able to purchase a fifty-thousand-guinea diamond should be living in a cottage.

The house had a stable, but my courage was all spent. I did not take the gig to it, but tethered the nag to the closest tree by means of the reins. My feet flew up the cobbled path to the door, with the welcoming light in the windows beyond. If there was a knocker, it was invisible by moonlight. I lifted my hand and knocked hard with my knuckles. A kindly-looking housekeeper in a dark gown and white cap answered within a minute.

"Is Mr. Kirby in, please?" I asked, my voice high from nerves too long stretched taut.

"He is, miss. Whom shall I say is calling?" she asked.

"Miss—Miss van Deusen," I told her, selecting the name he would recognize.

"Won't you come in?" she offered, holding the door wide.

I stepped into a simple country cottage. A fire lit the grate, throwing orange and yellow beams on the slate hearth, and the black cat stretched out at her ease there. The housekeeper offered me a seat, and returned a minute later with a glass of wine and three biscuits on a plate. Displeased with the interruptions, the cat left.

"Mr. Kirby is dressing, Miss van Deusen. He asked me to make you comfortable."

"Is he going out?" I asked, fearing he would slough me off without hearing my story.

"On the contrary, he has just come in. He will be down presently. There are papers and magazines on the table there, to pass the time."

With another friendly smile, she turned and left. I sipped the wine, and a moment later picked up the top newspaper, not that I was in any mood to read it. For a full minute, I did not even notice the language was not English. I had no idea what it was. While I was still frowning over the strange symbols, there was a heavy step beyond the archway. I looked eagerly to have my first view of the mysterious Mr. Kirby.

"Good evening, Miss van Deusen. It took you the deuce of a long time to get here," Major Morrison said, rather crossly.

"You!" I gasped. If I had arisen, I would surely have fallen over from shock and consternation. As I was already seated, I arose.

"As you see." He smiled an insouciant smile, bowed gracefully, and sauntered into the room.

"It was a trick! All a wicked lie!" I exclaimed, looking toward the door, but his wide shoulders blocked the exit very effectively.

"So it was, but what is a little deception between friends?
143

I see Mrs. Hunter has given you some wine. Have you had dinner? I hope not. I was about to sit down to mine, and would appreciate your company."

"I begin to understand your strategy now. You wanted me to come here so I wouldn't tell the police who stole the Jaipur. That's it. Don't bother to deny it."

"Why, the truth of the matter is, I didn't particularly want you to come at all. But as you are here, about dinner..."

"I wouldn't sit at your table if I were dying of starvation. You—you *liar!*"

"Harsh words, and from such a gentle little lamb too. Well, as you have been kind enough to sit at my fireside, I shall have Mrs. Hunter set me up a table here beside you." He called his housekeeper and asked her to put a card table at the other fireside chair. And still he did not budge from the door, but looked pointedly from me to it. "Don't even think of it, Anna. You are not going anywhere. You looked perfectly hagged. *Do* sit down and drink up your wine, like a good girl."

Fearful lest it was drugged or poisoned, I flung the contents of my glass into the fire. "Thank you for not tossing it into my face. I have just made a fresh toilette."

On that bold speech, he left the doorway, to sit on the arm of my chair, grabbing my wrists, to prevent my escape.

"What have you done with Mr. Kirby?" I demanded. My breaths came fast and shallow, as I felt those strong fingers dig into my flesh.

"Mr. Kirby has served his purpose. He became—expendable," he said, in a polite tone.

"You *killed* him!"

"In a word, yes."

I didn't doubt it for a minute, and as I considered his words, I knew the only purpose Kirby had served was to get my father to Glanbury Park, and myself to this cottage. "I see," I said.

"That is doubtful. Let me explain. Having you come here was preferable to having you break into jail to free your father. The authorities are so regimented in their thinking. They would be bound to take it amiss. There was the dreadful possibility too that you might announce to the press or even the law that I had stolen the Jaipur. Now don't deny it *occurred* to you! I know you well enough, Anna, to read you like an open book."

"So you lured me here."

"My real motive was to *lure* you—such a melodramatic turn of phrase you novel-reading ladies develop—into my lair and have my way with you. Isn't that what you are thinking?"

I tried to wrench my wrists from his grasp, for at the end of his speech, he did actually incline his head towards mine, groping for my lips.

"I knew I should have shaved it off," he said, shaking his head. "I very nearly did, but am not quite ready to execute Major Morrison yet."

"What do you.... Are you saying...?"

"That Mr. Kirby is one of my own alter egos? He is, or *was*. I don't think it will be necessary to resuscitate him. I like Major Morrison better, and old Kirby has served his purpose."

"He got my father to come down here and be accused of robbery, you mean?"

"That's one way of putting it. He also got the best gem expert in the kingdom to come and confirm there was some fishy business in connection with Lucien's collection. His own arrest was not foreseen, I promise you. That was not integral to my dastardly plot in the least. In fact, it added an unnecessary and very troublesome character to the story. You. But I have enjoyed having you around. You were useful, and entertaining—up to a point," he added judiciously, quirking his head to one side to examine me.

When Mrs. Hunter came to lay the table, she was accompanied by a young woman. "Perhaps you would be interested to meet Miss Little, Anna," Morrison asked, smiling lazily from one of us to the other. "Your predecessor at Glanbury Park."

Miss Little bobbed a curtsey and smiled, while I continued trying to sort out his bits of information. He had been working with Miss Little then.

"I read the feverish activity going forth behind your wrinkled brow," he informed me, with a mocking glance. He waited until Miss Little and Mrs. Hunter had moved the side table to his chair and placed a linen cloth on it and left, presumably for the food tray. "You are wondering, no doubt, how I have made use of little Miss Little for my foul ends. Let me clarify the matter. An expensive matter it was too, having to hire this cottage for her, but it has served for luring you as well, so I don't begrudge the expense in the least. I do just begin to wonder whether I ought not to have leased a larger place. My harem grows by leaps and bounds."

"Did *you* get her placed at the Park?"

"No, Algernon did, to keep an eye on things for him. I got her to leave." I shot a quick, suspicious look at this telling speech. "With Algernon's help. He sent her a note introducing me and requesting her to do as I asked. I asked her to take French leave for a while. To make room for you," he added swiftly. "When you came pelting to the Shipwalk, it was clear you meant to hang around the neighborhood, making a nuisance for me, and likely getting yourself thrown into the jail with your father. A lady can come to a shocking bad end with a reputation like that trailing her. So I—convinced Miss Little to leave, and bribed the servant at the Shipwalk to tell you of the vacancy so you would be hired before someone else beat you to the position. I could have just brought you directly here, of course, but thought you might be helpful to me at the Park. Having it to hold over your head that I knew who you were put you within my power more effectively than a Miss Little, on whom I had no real claims. You follow me? If your silence on any little matter should be necessary, I could always threaten to expose you. I rather feared you were going to create a fuss yesterday, when all my experts and I were busy convincing Beaudel the Jaipur was a fake. I am quite sure it was only your father's presence that deterred you."

"Are you saying it *wasn't* a fake?"

"Don't tell me Diamond Dutch's daughter can't see a diamond by daylight. Of course it wasn't a fake. It was magnificent."

"I don't believe you. My father would *never* lie about a thing like that."

"You actually *do* think I stole it then?" he asked, offended.

"Why are you trying so hard to confuse things, if you're not a thief?"

"Why do I just not state my true business, you mean, instead of assuming these various characters?"

"Exactly. And who are you anyway?"

"Complex problems seldom have simple solutions, Miss van Deusen. It is a famous quotation from someone or other, but I can't recall whom. Could you help me—with the identification, I mean?"

"No, and not with anything else either."

"Don't make me resort to force. I abhor it, especially with ladies."

"What did you plan to do if I hadn't come here?" I asked.

"You didn't mean to stand me up tonight? If I couldn't convince you to behave, I was going to abduct you from our trysting spot. I counted on your being discreet till you had an opportunity to talk to me, and if you were indiscreet, I hoped you would come here, as you did. I may be devious, but you must admit I am fairly thorough. Ah, dinner has arrived," he said, as Mrs. Hunter entered. "Are you sure you won't have something? The chicken looks delicious, Mrs. Hunter."

She bustled about, setting plates on the table, while I considered my means of escape. I thought it best to wait until the woman left, and he was busy with his meal.

When she left, and before he sat down, he said, "I took the precaution of having your gig and horse taken to the stable, where my groom is keeping an eye on them. Also on the back door, while I guard the front. You won't take a leap through one of the windows, will you, dear heart?"

On this speech, he sat down and took up his knife and fork. The loss of my gig meant darting through those black bushes alone, but on the other hand, night would help to hide me. "Quite sure you won't have anything?" he asked a moment later.

"Perhaps just a slice of bread and butter," I answered, seeing he would have to reach to the far side of his table for them. The few seconds might allow me to get out the front door, into the bushes.

"Ah good, you are coming down off your high ropes," he said, twisting in his chair, away from the door.

I lunged from my chair, pelted past him into the hall and wrenched the door open. A sharp expletive was heard in the room, then the sound of feet following fast behind me. I was out in the cool night air, flying toward the dense growth of bushes. He was still a few yards behind me when I hit the end of clear space, and was confronted with an impenetrable wall of brush, as high as my head. I pushed at it with my fingers, but could not make a path wide enough to enter. If I did, I would be scratched to pieces, and my progress would be too slow to allow any concealment. I felt his hands fall on my shoulders, spin me around, with his breaths heavy from the exertion of giving chase.

"You bloody fool! If you weren't a woman I'd..." He stopped, and glowered at me, still breathing hard, and looking very menacing, with the shadows of trees falling in bars across his upper face, the bottom of it swallowed up in blackness. I had the strongest expectation that, woman or not, I was about to receive a blow. Then he cocked back his head and laughed. His hand clamped me by one arm, and dragged me back into the house.

"Sit! And don't get up again till I've finished dinner," he commanded, actually shoving me into the chair. "Next time I may lose patience with you."

He resumed his seat, and kept a warier eye on me as he proceeded to make a good dinner, with many compliments to his absent cook, and more than one suggestion that I try a wing at least. It was a leisurely meal, with a second helping of apple tart and coffee afterwards. This necessitated a few trips back and forth by Mrs. Hunter. On the last one, she carried a cup and poured coffee for me. As it came from the same pot as the Major's, I accepted it. My lack of dinner was beginning to be felt.

"What are your plans for me?" I asked, as though it were a matter of only mild interest.

"Near future, or ultimately?" he enquired in the same spirit.

"Both."

"You will remain here for the time being."

"What explanation will you give at the Park?"

"I? Surely it is not my place to make excuses for a missing

governess. It is not a new experience for the Beaudels. They will cope."

"And my ultimate fate?"

"We all die sooner or later. That is the ultimate fate awaiting every man-jack of us."

"You are planning to murder me?"

"Only to kill you with kindness, my dear Anna. There would be no point in killing such a harmless enemy."

"What will you be doing with yourself, if I may enquire?"

"Feel free to make any enquiry you wish. I, of course, shall retain the prerogative to answer or not, as *I* wish. I shall humor you this time. I shall be busy winding up this nasty affair."

"Escaping with the Jaipur, you mean?"

"Incredible. Such faulty reasoning in a woman who passes for sane. Did I not have an opportunity to steal it when we were in the attic together? There was nothing but four small screws between me and it, as you know well. As to your being a witness, your high opinion of my morals surely does not preclude murdering you? It comes to seem a likely fate for you, sooner or later. No, I don't plan to steal it. I am going to protect it. You recall we discussed the possibility of Stella's having herself kidnapped, so that Beaudel would pay up the proceeds from the sale in ransom? I needed an excuse not to hand the blunt over to Beaudel, so claimed it was a fake. I also thought it a good idea to stir up the pot a little, set the crooks at each other's throats, as it were, and see what developed."

"What you have developed is a standstill."

"A standstill is come to, I believe, not developed, but you have fingered the flaw in the plan. We want not only to prevent Stella's grand larceny, but to reveal her for the hussy she is. She'll make a go for it sooner or later, and we want to be in on the affair. So we must give the pot another stir. Or even add a new ingredient."

"Another character?" I asked, entertaining the possibility he was a lesser evil than I had thought. At least his excuses had a sort of reason to them.

"No, another offer to purchase, but not the Jaipur. I believe Major Morrison will make an offer for the balance of the collection, and be ready to thwart Stella's efforts to get her hands on the loot."

"How will you do that?"

"Beaudel thinks she stole the diamond and substituted a fake, or so I hope."

"Yes, he does think it."

"He must learn her past history. I expect he has read the report of the attempted kidnapping of Kersey's son already, sent anonymously, of course. The name Wiggins figures prominently in it, along with the mention of a female accomplice. He's dumb, but not entirely stupid, and not entirely unscrupulous either. He was flattened to hear the diamond was a fake, but he still loves that baggage of a woman enough to protect her. He didn't call in the law, as he ought to have done. If he even half believed it was all Wiggins's doings, he might be convinced to save her life by paying the ransom, but if we can prove to him she is kidnapping herself, even he would not be fool enough to hand over the money."

"You'll have her watched, surreptitiously, to let Beaudel see she is involved?"

"Something like that. I haven't got all the details worked out. First I have to buy the remainder of the collection. I meant to explain all this to you tonight, at our tryst. I would have done so sooner, but events moved rather rapidly, after we both realized in the meadow that it was to be a kidnapping, and not theft pure and simple. I had to see Mills and coerce him to claim that a perfect jewel—wasn't it a *beauty?*—was a fake. There wasn't time, or later, opportunity, to tell you what I was about. You forgive me?"

"We'll make a deal."

"But of course I forgive you for thinking me a murderer, and for that ludicrous attempt to take French leave."

"Too kind, but that's not the deal. Tell me who you are."

"You can consider me a guardian angel, in disguise."

"An excellent disguise. I never saw an angel in a black beard and moustache before."

"How do they usually look, when you see them?"

"Blond and blue eyed," I answered gravely.

"That has been my experience also. I am going to the inn to speak to Mills. He will be with me tomorrow to look at the

Indian collection. Can I trust you to remain here, till I come back?"

"Certainly not. I'm going with you as far as the Park."

"The Park is not exactly on my way to Chelmsford."

"You will be happy for my help at the Park. It's not that far out of your way."

"I would rest easier knowing you are here, safe. Anything could happen tomorrow. There might, in the worst case, be gunshots."

"Then I should be there, to protect Lucien."

"Hmm, and I will be there to protect you, so I think I'll let you return, but do be careful."

When I was allowed to go back, I took it for proof Morrison was, if not an angel, at least on their side, but was still curious to know his identity. My gaze happened to fall on the newspaper with foreign writing. "What country is this from?" I asked, holding it up.

"India," he answered, then looked a trifle disconcerted. "We develop a dark tan in India, as you may have noticed."

"I seem to remember Beaudel mentioning Sacheverel had a son there."

He hunched his shoulders disparagingly. "A younger son. In fact, the baby of the family. I am not Papa's heir, alas. All that will go to my elder brother, but I have enough blunt to support an undemanding wife."

"I am sure that's the only sort who would ever marry you. Shall we go?"

A loudish laugh rang out. "Let's, before my patience breaks."

I went back in his carriage with him, the groom returning my gig behind us. "How did you get my father to go along with that story that the diamond was glass?"

"He knows the whole story. Finding the real thief will free him."

"What if this strategy doesn't work, Major?"

"Bertie is the name. If this doesn't work, then we'll come up with another stunt. I have dozens of ideas. Not to worry."

"If worst comes to worst, you can always try your charms on Stella again."

"Not an entirely unappetizing suggestion. She's a pretty

thing, but not bright. It would serve her well if she put herself to ransom and Beaudel didn't buy her back. There would be a pretty pickle. If he had any wits, he'd pay the hussy to stay away, but when December mates with May, there is no saying what weather will ensue."

"You'd better tell me the whole plan. Is that the idea, that you let her be kidnapped, and not pay to get her back?"

"That is up to Beaudel. We have to let him see with his own eyes that she is being voluntarily abducted. I have some hopes Wiggins will drag a ladder to her window, and she leap into his arms. It will be impossible for Beaudel to refute such evidence as that. Then we'll sit tight and wait for the ransom note."

"I wonder where he plans to take her—what place it was they had the Cantors hire. I wonder if she ever means to come back at all, after he pays."

"We may never have the satisfaction of knowing that, as they won't get the money."

"Will you have the law on hand, to witness the whole?"

"If my man in London is on his toes, there should be one of Townsend's boys at the inn waiting for me. I told him to send a Bow Street Runner along. I'll have to arrange some device for having him at the Park tomorrow. We can always use another authenticator of gems, if our imagination fails us. Or let on Sacheverel sent a footman to the house with some message or other. A very confidential letter from the old boy himself might account for a private messenger. Papa may have heard unsettling rumors, and be writing to question Beaudel."

"Poor Mr. Beaudel. It will be enough to give him a stroke. He wasn't far from it this afternoon."

"I felt badly to upset him so, but it is necessary to our success that he be sufficiently upset to turn against Madam Wife."

He had the carriage stopped at the edge of the main road, and walked with me up the walk, to prevent the sound of carriage wheels being heard in the house.

"How will you get inside?" he asked.

"By the kitchen door. It's nearly three hours since I left. I don't know what excuse to use, to explain my long absence."

152

"Where did you say you were going?"

"To town, to pick up something. I didn't say what."

"They'll think it was a young man. Let them. A stranger to the area, you took the wrong turn and went a few miles along the road, before discovering your error."

"I hope the gig is not far behind us. I can't go in without it."

"It can't be far behind. We set a slow pace. I wanted to have you all to myself for a while. Not that we took much advantage of the privacy. I think I hear Dobbin coming down the lane now."

When the gig caught up to us, I got in to take it around to the stable. "Come to our trysting window to let me know you got in without getting your ears boxed," he said.

"It won't be for a few minutes. I'll have to talk to cook for a while."

"See if she has anything of interest to tell us while you're at it. About what the Beaudels are up to, I mean, and the handsome butler."

Cook eyed me with the liveliest suspicion when I entered the kitchen. I asked if the Beaudels had been looking for me, and she said no.

"I'll go up and see that Lucien is settled in comfortably," I said, eager to get away before she started any hard questioning.

Tess was just coming down from the servants' quarters when I got upstairs. She assured me Lucien had gone to bed without any trouble. "The Beaudels didn't ask you about me?" I checked.

"Not they. They were downstairs billing and cooing till an hour ago, then they came up—together. They're in his room now. He looks like death in a jacket, but she's trying to cheer him up. I'm surprised she'd bother."

"Where's Wiggins?" I asked.

She smiled slyly. "Didn't he come home with you? *We* know you were with him, Miss Stacey. The two of you darting out ten minutes apart, with no explanation. You're a fast worker. I've been rolling my eyes at him any time these six months."

I cast down my eyes in a maidenly way, to encourage her along this line of thinking. I now had two choice bits of in-

153

formation for my accomplice. Before I went to the door to see him, I went into my room for a moment. I was exhausted from the exertions of the day. I was also very hungry, and still worried about my father. It also occurred to me that the son, even the youngest son, of Lord Sacheverel would have no serious interest in a merchant's daughter. He enjoyed romance and melodrama, the theatrical gesture, but I must not let my head be turned. When he had finished his business here, he would go back to his father's castle, and I to my father's hired rooms on Upper Grosvenor Square.

A quick glance at the reflection in the mirror did little to renew my confidence. I looked as hagged as he had told me I looked. I braced myself for one final exertion before the day was done. He was waiting at the door.

"You made it. Good. Any trouble?" he asked.

"None. Wiggins accidentally provided me with an excuse. They think I was with him. I wonder where he really was."

"Conspiring with the Cantors, perhaps."

"Stella has spent the evening reinstalling herself in Beaudel's good graces, so he'll be sure to ransom her. She's with him now, in his bedchamber."

"Have you been peeking in keyholes, Anna?" he asked, laughing.

"Certainly not. Tess told me. Servants all keep an eye on their master and mistress."

"We must remember that. One doesn't want his servants keeping too close an eye on him. We'll stuff the keyholes with sealing wax."

"I assure you that won't be necessary," I said, shocked at his free talk, and too tired to find it amusing.

"That's what you think. I don't want any chits of servants spying on us. Puts ideas into their heads. They're hard enough to keep in line as it is. Of course we won't have so handsome a butler as Wiggins."

"We're not——"

"No, we're not, and it's time we were. I'm already late for my appointment." On this speech he pulled me beyond view of the door and tried to kiss me. I struggled against him, becoming angry. Gentlemen did not take this form of freedom with ladies, not ones they were serious about. He mistook my

154

reaction for coquettishness, or modesty, and overcame my resistance. I was crushed in a passionate embrace that went on and on, until I forgot the implicit insult, the possibility of being seen by a prying servant, or any external consideration. For those moments, the world stopped at the perimeter of his arms. Inside it was a tumultuous ecstasy. He was worth the coiffeur, and the powdered nose, but they would be of no avail. Lord Bertie wasn't serious about Diamond Dutch's daughter. I pushed him away, and heard a hiccup, or sob, escape my bruised lips.

"Anna, what's the matter?" he exclaimed, staring at me, puzzled.

"You—everything. I—I'm worried about my father," I added, as an excuse for my condition.

He closed his arms around me, but gently, soothingly. "Poor girl, you have been through the mill. And I haven't helped either, have I? I didn't mean to vex you so."

I swallowed down my feelings, willed them to abeyance, until he was gone. "I'm overwrought. I have to get to bed."

"And I have to leave you—again. It becomes harder to do each time I'm with you. *Au revoir*."

"As they say in *Paris*," I added sarcastically.

"Actually I haven't been to Paris yet. Nice spot for a honeymoon, I should think. Happy dreams." He waved a kiss. "By the bye, did I remember to tell you what I found out?"

"What's that?"

"What we were discussing the other day, about kerseymere. It has nothing to do with Kersey, but is a corruption of cassimere. I told you I would look into it. Ah good, you are smiling. That's how I like to leave you."

Chapter Fifteen

After a disturbed, unsatisfactory sleep, I awoke next morning to be greeted by dull gray skies. There was no unusual bustle of activity going on at Glanbury Park. Lucien and I breakfasted in the nursery, as usual.

"Is anything interesting happening downstairs?" I asked Tess, when she brought the tray.

"Missing your beau, are you, Miss Stacey?" she answered with a pert smile. "You'll be happy to hear Wiggins is sitting in the kitchen polishing silver, looking every bit as blue as you do yourself. Where did you two go last night?"

"I didn't say I was with Wiggins," I answered primly.

"No, and didn't say he came in the back door not ten minutes after you either, but I have eyes in my head. I can see a romance going on underneath my very nose."

She tossed her saucy head and left. As I ate, it occurred to me that unless the weather cleared, I would not be able to see Bertie, whom I could not think of as anyone but the major, in the meadow that day. Depending on the hour he was to come to the Park, he might not be at our usual assignation, which cast a cloud over my breakfast. When Tess came to remove the tray, she was smiling.

"Wait till you see the caller just arrived," she exclaimed. "I may not bother trying to steal Wiggins from you. I think I like Sacheverel's messenger better. Not nearly so handsome, but more gallant, I think. He'll be coming up to see Master Lucien. He has a present for you, lad."

I felt Morrison had arranged the present to allow the Bow Street Runner an excuse to speak to myself, and was highly curious to hear what he had to say.

When a young man dressed in dark green livery entered the room, I was surprised, though of course some disguise was necessary.

"Mullins, from Danely Hall," he said, bowing. He was of medium height, with a shaggy crop of reddish curls. He must have exercised some outstanding gallantry toward Tess, to have weaned her affection from the handsome Wiggins. I smiled to see how ill his livery fitted him. There was room for two of him in the jacket. It was strange to think of Major Morrison having liveried servants at his beck and call. He had not the pompous air one associates with the nobility.

"Your grandpa sent you this here gift, boy," he said, stuffing a wrapped parcel into Lucien's eager hands. The boy sat at the table to unwrap it, leaving me free to beckon the Runner to a corner for some private conversation.

"You are a friend of Mr. Townsend, I believe?" I asked.

"That's it, miss. The major sent me to have a look about the premises. Have you noticed aught amiss?"

"Nothing, but I haven't been downstairs."

"The Mrs. is all but spooning his tea into the old fellow. It might be as good a time as any to have a look about her room."

"What for?" I asked.

"Clues," he answered grandly. "To find out where the place is they hired, and if she has a bit of a bag packed up."

Without more talk, he slithered out the door, as though he hadn't a bone in his body. He moved glidingly, like water. After scanning the hallway for traffic, he asked me to point

157

out her chamber. He flowed to it, and soon disappeared from sight. While awaiting his return, I went to praise Lucien's present. It was a boxed set of animals, carved in ivory. I smiled to think of Bertie's thoughtfulness in having brought them from India for his nephew. Lucien was busy setting out dainty elephants, tigers, horses, dogs and other specimens.

"I don't know whether to make a zoo or a jungle," he said, staring at them, and moving them about. "Which shall we make, Miss Stacey?"

"We don't want the poor creatures locked up. Let them roam free, as they did in India. It was thoughtful of your Uncle Bertie to—send them to you."

"I don't have any Uncle Bertie," he told me. "It is my Uncle Sheldon who is in India, and he never sends me anything. He doesn't even know me."

"You must be mistaken!" I exclaimed, thrown into confusion.

He looked at me as though I were mad, or a moron. "I know my own uncles' names, Miss Stacey. Yes, I shall make a jungle. We'll get some plants from the park," he decided, but in the interim he was content to let the crushed brown wrapping be their lair, and I had to be content to assure myself Sheldon, for some reason, preferred the nickname of Bertie.

I hovered near the door, craning my neck out to look for Mullins, or more precariously, Mrs. Beaudel or a servant going to her chamber.

My vigil was soon rewarded. Mullins's carrot top peeped out from the door, then glided towards me. "She has nothing packed. She could hardly do so. It would be as good as a declaration she knew what was to happen."

"Nothing to tell you where the hired house is either?"

"Not in plain view. I hadn't time to give it a good rifle. I'll slip below and watch her. If she comes upstairs, you are to keep your eyes sharp, Miss, and your ears. If you hear her window slide open, or anything of a suspicious nature, dart down to the kitchen and notify me. Keep a lookout on the yard as well," he added, flowing to the window. "Aye, this is as good a spot as any for you to stay today."

"Do you know what time Morrison is coming?" I asked.

"He's sending a note asking for an interview at two. If it is not granted, he will let me know. We figure the snatch will be made right after his visit, when she knows Beaudel has got the check in his fingers."

"You don't think they might wait a few days, Mullins?"

"Nay, it would complicate matters, if he got the blunt invested and then had to pull it out. It takes time. They'll strike while the iron is hot. Time's running out for them, with this Sir Algernon fellow coming home soon."

This forecast made a tedious day for me, sitting cooped up in the nursery, with not even my rendezvous in the meadow. "You'll look out for Wiggins below?" I asked.

"That I will. The lad's as nervous as a cat on a griddle. He's polished the same teapot three times. Not a bit happy to see me land in on him either, but I don't believe he suspects anything amiss. I've been prosing his ears off with stories from Sacheverel's place."

"Morrison supplied you with an ill-fitting suit from Danely Hall," I mentioned, wondering if the runner knew Morrison was in reality Lord Sheldon.

"He didn't supply it. Bow Street has a wardrobe. Morrison just told us the color. The buttons ain't right, he says, but they'd not know that here."

"Morrison, of course, would know," I said, hoping for some confirmation from Bow Street that he was indeed Sacheverel's son.

"Aye," he said, but in an unthinking way.

"What excuse have you made for remaining the whole day?" I asked.

"There was questions in the letter I brought that want answers. The old gent is in the fidgets, and hasn't got round to writing his reply up yet. It would make no sense to set out in the afternoon, so it looks as though I've got my excuse right and tight."

We went to the table and chatted to Lucien for a while. Mullins was soon in charge of the elephant and some smaller animals, concealing them in folds of the brown paper, to repel attack from the tiger and hyena.

He was running up and down from kitchen to nursery all

159

that morning. On one visit, he informed me Morrison's letter had come, and Beaudel had agreed to the hour for the visit.

"How did you find out?" I asked.

"We have our ways, Miss," he said grandly. "If you're interested in the business at all, what I done is this. I lingered at the end of the hallway when I saw the letter arrive, and within ten minutes the old boy rung for Wiggins. Wiggins went straight to the kitchen and give a footboy a letter to go to the Shipwalk. So was it a yes or no, you are thinking. I know it was telling the major to come ahead, for Wiggins said he'd best get on with his silver polishing, as Beaudel was expecting a caller at two, and he'd have to be out of his apron to catch the door. Induction, you see. Or possibly deduction, but plain logical thinking is the trick."

The skies cleared as the long morning progressed. On different trips, Mullins informed me that Beaudel had locked his office door, which his logical thinking told him the collection was being removed and examined. He had seen Mrs. Beaudel talking to Wiggins, a lively discussion he described it, and took it for an omen of the pending kidnapping. At lunch, he brought up the tray for Tess, which no doubt raised him even higher in her esteem.

"I've had a word from Morrison. We agreed beforehand I'd saunter out to the stable at eleven, to pass on my report to him, and hear what he had to say, if anything. He's decided you can take the wee lad down to the meadow as you usually do. 'Twill be better to have you and him out of the way of possible harm, do you see?"

"But I was going to help—help spy for him."

"You've already done that. We wouldn't want no harm to come to the lad, now would we, miss?"

"No, of course not," I said reluctantly.

"There'll be *me* here, to see her sneaking out of the house by her own volition, and report same to Bow Street at the proper time, so you take the lad out, as the major advises."

I had been listening to hear if Mullins ever referred to Morrison as Lord Sheldon, and noticed he had not. I decided it was time to clarify it, and set my mind at rest. "Did Lord Sheldon ask you to refer to him as Major Morrison?" I asked.

"We agreed it was for the best. It's the name he goes by

in this house, and to make sure I don't let anything slip to the contrary, I just call his lordship Major."

"How did he prove to you that he actually *is* Sacheverel's son?"

"Why bless my soul, he never proved nothing to *me*, ma'am. He dealt with Mr. Townsend direct. He satisfied the chief, and that's got to be good enough for me. Have you doubts, then?" he asked, with quick interest.

"Just curious."

"Ah, 'tis an interesting business, being with Bow Street. Folks always *do* ask us a million questions, how we trap criminals and all. Logic—there's the secret."

It seemed hard to miss the excitement after my tedious morning, but Lucien's safety was paramount, and in the end I agreed to it.

There was one opportunity to gauge Mrs. Beaudel's mental state for myself. She went to her room to freshen herself for luncheon, and stopped in at the nursery for a moment.

"I hear your Uncle Sacheverel sent you a gift, Lucien," she said, her muddy green eyes searching the room for it. "Carved animals. How pretty they are. Sheldon must have sent them to you from India."

"No, Lord Sacheverel sent them to me himself," he replied, fondling the tiger.

"What do you call him?" she asked, tousling his curls.

"I don't have a name for him," he said, gently removing her hand.

"Bring them down to the saloon tonight to show your Uncle Charles, and we shall make names for them all, like Adam and Eve naming the animals," she suggested, with a fond smile.

What an actress she was, to smile and beam, while planning to rob the boy.

"They already have that kind of names," he told her. "I think I will call the tiger Algernon, after my brother."

"Why don't you make the hyena Algernon?" she asked, her smile fading, as she turned to me. "He looks a little pale, don't you think, Miss Stacey? But you will be taking him out this afternoon, as usual?"

"Yes, we always go out on fine days."

"I think I will call the peacock after you, Aunt Stella," Lucien said, but with no intention of irony or ill will. The peacock was a pretty, dainty bird.

"Goose! A peacock is the male of the species, and I do not wish to be a peahen. I wish we had some peacocks for the park. I wonder how people get them to stay where they want them. Dear me, look at the time. I must dash. You *will* take Lucien out this afternoon? I don't like to see my little guy's color fading."

"Yes, I will."

She left. I thought she seemed nervous, more fidgety and chattering than usual. Small wonder!

At fifteen to two, I got my pelisse and took Lucien down the servants' stairs, to leave by the back door. Mullins sat in the kitchen, enjoying a small ale. When we came down, he arose and sauntered in a casual-seeming way toward the stairs, to take up his vigil above. Wiggins was also there, having Tess give his shoulders a final brushing, before going abovestairs to greet Major Morrison and Mr. Mills.

"Time for your ride, is it?" Cook asked Lucien.

"I am not riding today. I am going to collect a jungle for my animals. Have you got a box I can use? A good big box."

"A jungle? My, I haven't got anything that big!"

"The box the sugar and tea come in will do. It will only be a small jungle, Cook," he told her, with a very superior air.

"If it's only twigs and grass you're after, I fancy this little box will do you," she said, rummaging in a corner for a small-ish box.

From the meadow, one has a fine view of the back of Glanbury Park. On that particular afternoon, it was the east side I wished to see. If a ladder went up to Mrs. Beaudel's window, or if she let herself down by a rope, I did not mean to miss it. It struck me then, in the clear afternoon sunlight, that a daytime kidnapping was not at all a likely thing. They would wait until darkness fell. Beaudel was not going to get the money invested in an hour. Arrangements with brokers and so on would take a few days. Lucien was soon busy pulling out weeds and newly sprouted trees to form his jungle, while

162

I sat on the grass, staring at the east side of the building, where there was not a single suspicious thing happening.

When he had collected his jungle, Lucien decided he would go to the stream to stir up the tadpoles. I was to guard his jungle box. My eyes went in slow arcs from stream to window, back and forth, back and forth, until I was tired of doing it. What a lack of logic on Mullins's part, and Morrison's too, to think anyone would be stupid enough to have herself kidnapped in midafternoon, when a few hours would lend her darkness and privacy. I was so certain the deed would be done at night that I got up to go and tell Mullins so.

I looked back to the stream to call Lucien, and saw no sight of him. It was less than a minute, not more than thirty seconds, since I had seen his black head bobbing at the stream's edge. He was just bending over, I decided, and went to fetch him, my mind still more occupied with the other matter. Possibly Mullins and Morrison thought Stella would take her departure when Beaudel went to the bank to deposit the money. That was why they were alert in broad daylight. I called to Lucien, as I approached the stream, still looking about for him. I began to fear he had fallen in, and hastened my pace. There was no answer to my shouts. I looked all around, and saw only some trampled grass where he had been. Beyond the stream, at this point, there was thin brush. A few branches were still swaying, where he had pushed his way in. A rabbit or fox had caught his attention, I thought, annoyed.

"Lucien!" I called. "Come back. We're going in." There was no answer.

That was my first apprehension of anything amiss. He was not badly behaved. He would have answered at least, if he had not wanted to come just yet. I called again, louder, and again heard nothing but the gentle swishing of the leaved branches, then a quiet sound of running feet. Without thinking, I leaped across the stream and pushed my way into the tangle of brush, just at the point where the branches had been moving. Ahead of me, in the clearing, I saw a woman dressed in black, walking at a quick, awkward gait, hurrying, with some heavy burden in her arms. As I looked and shouted, she turned and peered over her shoulder at me. It was Mrs.

163

Cantor, the milliner from the village. There was no mistaking her black eyes. She wore an expression that would have curdled cream. It was not the expression that turned my blood to water though. It was the little black shoes protruded from one side of her bundle, and the black head glimpsed from the other side. She was carrying Lucien in her arms, an inert bundle. He was unresisting, obviously unconscious. I couldn't even allow myself to think the other—that he was dead.

A wild scream, my own, rent the still air, as I took flight after her. I didn't get farther than three steps before a heavy blow fell across my temple. I saw an arm in a dark coat, with a gloved hand at its end, holding some sort of stick or stone, swing past my face, just at the corner of vision. Then darkness and oblivion came over me.

Chapter Sixteen

It was a cellar they took us to, not a large one, but a small, dark, damp, moldy cave of a place, containing nothing but our own bodies and a pile of coal in a corner. It was too dark to read my watch, but I had the instinctive feeling that not a great deal of time had passed since I was knocked on the head in the meadow. As soon as I realized I was not dead and gone to hell, I began feeling in the darkness for Lucien, praying he was here, and not buried. He was lying beside me, wriggling like a pig in a basket. I was surprised to discover I had not been tied. They counted on the blow to keep me unconscious until we were securely locked in this hole, it seemed.

"Are you hurt, Lucien?" I asked. A muffled sound came from his head.

Feeling around, I found a gag binding his mouth, and removed it.

"We have been kidnapped, Miss Stacey!" he said, his voice

sounding hollow in the cave, and not entirely displeased at such dashing goings on. "By daylight! If Algernon hears of it, he will think me a flat. Did they hurt you?"

"Yes, my head hurts where they hit me, but I'm all right. No bones broken," I replied in a low voice. "Whisper, in case they are listening nearby."

"My hands and feet are tied up," he told me.

I fumbled until I discovered the ropes, but in the darkness it was hard to undo the tight knots. It was a fine cord, but very strong. It seemed an eternity before I managed to work the wrist bindings loose. "I will get the ones off my ankles myself," Lucien told me. With my fingernails in shreds, I let him do it.

"The first thing we have to do is find the door," he chattered on as he worked, speaking in low tones.

There were small, scrabbling sounds coming from the corners of the cave, suggesting the presence of rodents. My own instinct was to stay away from the corners, but as soon as he got his bonds loose, Lucien stood up and started prowling about, very softly.

"Don't be afraid, Miss Stacey. I'll take care of you," he told me, in a reassuring way.

"You must be very quiet, Lucien. If you feel a door, don't jiggle the handle."

"I will listen at the keyhole first. There's stairs here," he said, excited. "I'll go up. There must be a door." I followed him to the foot of the stairs, waited with my heart pounding while he made his ascent, and came back down again. "There *is* a door, with a doorknob."

"I'll try the knob, very quietly," I told him, and crept up the dark steps, feeling my way. First I listened, hearing nothing but silence beyond. The knob made no sound as I turned it. It was not locked, but it was bolted firmly on the other side. We were locked into a cellar somewhere in the pitch black, with no notion where we might be, and no means of escape. I went back down the stairs and sat on the floor with Lucien, trying to fight off the panic.

"I hope you are not frightened," he said, his little hand finding its way into mine. His voice was beginning to show signs of strain.

"Just a little," I confessed.

"Why do you think they kidnapped us?"

"For ransom money, Lucien. That is why people are kidnapped. You must not worry. Your uncle will pay them, and we will be allowed to go home."

"He won't pay much for you, Miss Stacey," he felt obliged to inform me.

"No, I don't suppose he will."

"I will make him rescue you, after they send me home."

"Thank you," I said, biting back a worried smile.

"What should we do now?"

"Let us just sit here a moment and think."

That is when we discovered the only thing in the room other than ourselves and the mice was a great pile of coal. I preferred to sit on the coal than on the floor, so that is what we both did. Lucien pretended to be chilly, to give him an excuse to cuddle up against me. I put my arm around him, and we sat together in the dark, thinking.

"How long will it be before I am rescued?" he asked.

"Not too long, I hope. A few hours—maybe tonight."

"I am hungry already."

"It's not long since lunch. Why don't you try to rest—sleep?"

"I think I should be making plans," he countered.

He didn't sleep, but he was quiet, which gave me the opportunity to cudgel my brains, and curse my stupidity at not thinking it might be Lucien who was kidnapped after all, as I had first thought. I wondered who the man was who helped Mrs. Cantor. Probably her husband. It wasn't Wiggins at any rate. But it was Wiggins and Stella who had engineered it. They had not meant for me to see Mrs. Cantor. Lucien was to have been carried off alone. But Lucien knew Mrs. Cantor too. Without seeing her, he could not positively identify her, however.

"Did you see the woman who snatched you up?" I asked.

"No, somebody hit my head and when I woke up, it had a bag over it. It was dirty. When we were in the carriage, somebody tied up my arms and legs. I felt them do it, but I didn't say anything. I wonder why they covered my head. Maybe to hide where they were taking us."

"You have no idea where we are?" I confirmed, wondering if we were in the cellar of the millinery shop at the edge of the village.

"I know where we are not. I peeked up under the edge of the bag when the carriage jostled me. I got one look out the window, and I didn't see anything I knew. I know all the houses on the way to the town."

"What did you see?"

"Just bushes, growing close to the road."

"No buildings at all?"

"No, but don't worry, Miss Stacey. Major Morrison will rescue us."

"I hope so," I agreed, but a worse idea was taking root in my mind. It was Major Morrison who had suggested I take Lucien to the meadow in the first place. It was Morrison who had got my father involved in the whole mess, and was active every step along the way since, as I muddled deeper and deeper into it. For that matter, I had only Major Morrison's word for it that Wiggins and Stella had ever kidnapped any-one. Only his word for it that he was Sacheverel's son, mys-teriously called Bertie, when the man's name was Sheldon. Worst of all, Morrison had a place hired the size of whose cellar must approximate the size of this one, and whose access road was lined with bushes. He was involved with Miss Little, and I had seen him with my own eyes making love to Stella. He was one of them. He seemed genuinely fond of Lucien, but then the plan did not call for killing Lucien, only robbing him. Lucien had not seen his abductors—he could be set free when they had the money. I could not. A longer perusal of the facts pointed out one startling inconsistency—Morrison had paid the money that was to be used for ransom, so what was the point in it all? What had he gained? The rose Jaipur? It seemed an unnecessarily involved plan, but to find him innocent was even more complicated, with so much evidence against him.

We remained in the cellar all night without food or drink, or anyone so much as coming to the door to see if we were alive or dead. Mercifully, Lucien fell asleep, and slept for what seemed to me like several hours. I walked all around the room, feeling the ceiling with my hands, in hopes of finding a trapdoor. There was none—nothing but dirt and cobwebs. When he awoke, we talked quietly for a while. He complained of hunger, and I assured him we would soon have food, but my own greater need was for water. My throat was dry and cracked. At some time during that long black afternoon and night, I too dozed off for a few hours. I was awakened by the sound of the bolt being drawn on the other side of the door at the top of the stairs. I looked, frightened to death, to see who it was, but saw no more than a pair of shoes and a skirt, with some light shining behind. I crawled closer to check that it was Mrs. Cantor, and saw a masked face. The shock of it nearly killed me—to see a piece of sheeting with two holes cut for eyes. She was doing it so Lucien could not positively identify her, of course. She swung a lantern to and fro, examining us to see we were still alive. I took advantage of the brief illumination to look around our cellar. All I saw was the extent of the coal pile, that nearly reached the ceiling. I knew well enough the futility of quizzing her.

"Who are you?" Lucien asked, his voice a pitiful squeak of terror. He was trembling, and I was not far from it myself.

"Breakfast," the woman said, in a voice distorted to hide its true sound. She took a tray from a table, put it on the top step, banged the door and slid the bolt.

"I expect it is bread and water," Lucien said, his voice quavering. He was familiar with the ways of villains, from his books.

It was slightly better than he prophesied. Two rough chunks of bread each, and a cup of tea, but we were hungry and dry enough to consume every iota of both, with never a thought until they were gone that they might contain poison, or a sedative.

"I am still hungry," Lucien said in a small voice.

"Never mind, my dear, it is morning now, and soon we will be rescued."

He talked on about the mask, and the reason for it, and finally accepted my opinion that she was trying to frighten us. I am convinced a child would find amusement in a flaming house. Before long, he was climbing up the coal pile and sliding down. He was at this when Mrs. Cantor, still masked, came for the tray. With her stage voice, she told me to leave it on the top step then return below, which I did, as she carried a butcher knife. As soon as I came down, she took the tray and bolted the door.

"Ouch!" Lucien exclaimed suddenly, in a loud voice.

"Be careful, Lucien," I cautioned.

"There's something sharp in here," he said.

I ran forward to feel in the blackness with my fingers, hoping for a weapon—an axe, a shovel. There was a sharp edge of tin, but it could not be dislodged. It was attached to something. I pushed the coal aside, to follow the contours of the thing, a sort of large, rough tray it felt like. Its end was buried a foot in the coal pile, and above, it continued for several feet. I had to climb up the coal heap like Lucien to follow its path. It went right to the top of the wall.

I was confused as to what it could be, until I reached the end, at the outer wall of the house, and realized it was a coal chute. The coal was put into the cellar from the yard beyond, to save carrying bags of coal into the house and down the steps. I was weak with hope, as I considered there must be some opening, some covered hole, to allow the coal down the slide. I explored carefully with my fingers, feeling a sharp, circular ridge of metal. Without too much effort, it slid softly out, to land on the ground outside. A weak ray of light penetrated the gloom. How welcome it was! Columbus could not have been happier to spot America. I shushed Lucien, who was babbling excitedly, and clambering up the coal pile beside me.

We peered together through the hole, our tunnel of vision showing us a patch of earth where a few blades of grass had sprung up. Beyond the clearing there was a spinney, a rough expanse of thicket. If it was not the thicket surrounding Mr. Kirby's house in the country, it was one very like it. My first excitement died away as I realized the hole was too small to let us escape. And it was not likely anyone but our captors would walk within shouting distance of it. Still, it was good to see the light again, to feel a breeze fan our cheeks, to know the real world was still spinning out there, waiting for us. It gave courage to struggle on.

"I think *I* could squeeze out that hole. I am very small," Lucien said.

"You'd never make it," I said, measuring the space with my eyes against his shoulders.

"I *know* I could," he insisted, pushing his head through the metal-lined hole. It was about eight inches in depth, the thickness of the walls of the house.

"I don't want you to get stuck," I said, to dampen his enthusiasm, and pulled him back.

He again wriggled his way into the opening, bracing his feet against my hips. When he got his shoulders through, I knew the thing was done. To this day, I don't know how he did it, though I have seen dogs wiggle their way through holes much smaller than they. There was a deal of wriggling and squiggling, as he hunched his shoulders into the smallest possible size, then edged through, his little feet kicking behind him, as I shoved gently, with a silent prayer to God above. Soon he was crouched on the ground outside, smiling in at me, his face as black as the ace of spades from his confinement in the coal hole. His whole suit was grimed like a chimney sweep's.

The next item was for him to go for help. Sending him to Glanbury Park was risky. If Stella or Wiggins saw him before he reached his uncle, he might end up back in the coal hole, or in some other prison. Major Morrison was a doubtful conspirator. The constable, I thought, was our safest bet. But where were we? How far had he to go, and in what direction? He might well be picked up as a runaway Parish child, the condition he was in. All this had to be considered and a decision taken in a second, lest our captors glance out the window and see him.

"I'll go and get the major," he said.

"No! No, Lucien, go to the police."

"Major Morrison would do a better job."

"I—I believe he had to go to London," I said, to change his mind.

"Then I will go to the police."

"Hurry. Hurry, and be careful. I don't know which direction, but cut through the spinney and stop at the first farmhouse you come to. Tell them what happened, and to send for the police. Let the police tell your Uncle Charles."

"I will be back soon. I'll bring you some food, Miss Stacey," he promised, and was gone, with the wits to crouch low as he darted into the concealing safety of the spinney. I rather thought the thicket around Morrison's country place was more dense, but then a child was low to the ground, and the brush would be thinner there. I watched until he disappeared, then sat at the open hole, wishing I had asked him to return the lid, in case anyone passing on the other side should see it, and suspect our trick. I tried to reach it by sliding my arm through the opening, but between the shifting of the coal heap beneath me and the distance to the ground, I had no luck. I marveled anew how Lucien had made it out that tiny orifice, then sat on thorns, worrying, and waiting for his return with a rescuer. My only hope of avoiding death was a six-year-old boy, who didn't even know where he was, or where he was going.

Chapter Seventeen

I watched and waited at my lookout hole for hours. At least I knew what time it was now. As my watch showed twelve noon, I piled coal up in front of the hole, as I did not want Mrs. Cantor to see it open. Then I sat waiting, but she did not come. After a few hours, I realized lunch was to be omitted. I was hungry enough to gnaw on a chunk of coal, but again the thirst was worse. No sound of coming or going was heard beyond the hole. It seemed probable the access route to the stable was on this side of the house, where the coal cart obviously came in. I couldn't get my head through the hole to look. The eight-inch thickness of the wall defeated me. Only a giraffe could have done it, or a Lucien.

As the afternoon wore on, I became extremely worried that he had been captured. If he had got free, help would have reached me before now. I envisaged Lucien, locked up alone in some other place, or some other room of this same house. How frightened he would be, poor brave tyke. He wouldn't have to disguise his fear if he were all alone. I couldn't forget either that my own case was worse. I wondered in what manner they would dispose of me. Would I be left here to starve, then rot? In some distant future, a skeleton in a navy blue gown would be found, sitting on top of a coal heap. Would anyone even remember the governess who had disappeared with Lucien Beaudel, and connect her with my bones?

Weak from hunger, cramped from sitting, and fatigued with worry, I decided to sleep, and covered the hole with coal again, in case of a visitor. When I awoke, I shoved the coal away to see the hour. The sun was just setting, which told me my lookout faced the west. It was the direction Lucien had run to, but I had no idea in which direction Glanbury Park or Chelmsford lay. With nothing else to do, I decided to try the door again, on the chance it had been left unbarred. As I approached the top of the stairs, I saw the dim outlines of another tray. She had come while I slept, and left it without awakening me. So I was not to be starved to death after all. I noticed two cups on the tray, and two bowls of perfectly cold stew, two spoons. Then they didn't know Lucien had gotten out. She had seen me stretched out on the coal pile and thought he was with me, sleeping. Her lamp was dim enough to make that mistake, I realized, with a new rush of hope. But what was taking him so *long?*

My hunger welcomed the double servings. I ate Lucien's stew and my own, drank our tea, grateful for the liquid, cold and unsugared though it might be. Then I placed the tray at the bottom of the step, and sat scheming how I could overpower her when she came for it. Maybe a large block of coal.... But there was none large enough to knock her unconscious, so I took it up and placed it on the side of the top step, in case she asked Lucien to take it to her. I felt better after eating. Back to my perch, to sit at the hole and watch the sun set. It was red and bright and beautiful, then it was suddenly gone. The shadows turned to purple, then by degrees to black space. Once it was dark, there was no worry about the hole being seen. I could just sit and listen and wait.

One loses all track of time, alone in the dark. I was not tired, and not entirely despondent. Lucien might yet bring help to me. Every night sound was magnified to my listening ears. I knew we were removed some distance from the main road, as I heard no noise of traffic passing. This made the sound, when finally it came, more significant. In an anguish of waiting, I heard the fast clipping of a team draw near, saw a darker shadow in the gloom as it passed by, to stop a few yards beyond my listening spot. It would be a constable, or Mr. Beaudel, or some kindly farmer brought by Lucien. When at last a human voice was heard, my spirits sank. It was Stella Beaudel. The heavier tread that accompanied hers would certainly be Wiggins.

A light, teasing laugh wafted toward me, from above. "But however did you manage to *steal* it, Major?" Stella asked. "The Jaipur is worth a huge sum."

"A trade secret, my dear Stella. I suppose you have the boy here too, have you?"

"Ask me no questions, I'll tell you no lies. What do you mean to do with her? Eventually, I mean, for I know your plans for the near term."

"I can handle Miss Stacey. She won't be any problem."

Their footfalls stopped not more than a yard past my listening port. My heart stood still. One of them must have seen the hole cover, lying on the ground. Her gurgling laugh soon disabused me of this idea. "Tch, tch. Remember I am a married woman," she said seductively, but her very tone was an invitation to forget it. The long silence that ensued indicated he had accepted her invitation. What else could they be doing in the dark, except embracing?

What sense was to be made of what I had heard? He was working with them, yet not entirely in their confidence. He did not know where they had taken Lucien. How then did he know *I* was here? And in what manner did he intend to "handle" me? Had it something to do with my father, my silence for his freedom? Or was it something more menacing than that? They didn't know Lucien had escaped. That was my trump card, and I figured how to play it. Forget that Morrison *had* stolen the Jaipur. Of course my father would never have lied about that diamond being glass. I shouldn't have doubted him for a moment, or trusted Morrison for a second. I squeezed my eyes shut and uttered a brief, silent prayer.

They would be at the door in seconds. I slid down from the

top of the coal pile just as sounds were heard at the top of the stairs. The lantern that was soon swinging there, waist high, showed the fawn-trousered legs and topboots of the major, and behind them a gleam of green satin that was Stella's skirt. She stood back, to prevent Lucien from seeing her.

"Come up, Miss Stacey," Morrison commanded imperially.

As I took a step forward, he came down one step, knocking the tray askew. Stella handed him the lantern, then stepped back further. "I might as well see if the boy is all right while I'm here," he said nonchalantly. There was a low murmur of disapproval from Stella, but he advanced. "How is he? Is he awake?" he asked.

He held the lantern up toward my face to examine me. "Good God!" he gasped, giving me some idea what the coal hole had done to my appearance. His eyes were wide, his mouth open in shock. "Where's Lucien?" he asked, when he had recovered.

"Lucien? How should *I* know? He's not here," I answered blandly, tossing the cat amongst the pigeons, to see what would transpire. Morrison's free hand grasped my upper arm, squeezing it.

"Not here? What are you talking about? Of course he's here!" Stella proclaimed, and flew down the stairs to see for herself that he was not. Shock and dismay robbed her of caution.

Morrison looked at her with a sharp frown, then made a quick tour of the basement. The merciful shadows obliterated the small hole through which he had escaped. Even the breeze conspired by dropping, so as not to betray its presence.

"What have you done with him?" Stella demanded, her eyes accusing.

"Don't be ridiculous! What *could* she have done? There's no place to hide him," Morrison said.

"I haven't seen him since yesterday afternoon," I declared without a tremor.

"Mrs. Cantor!" Stella turned and fled up the stairs.

"Where is he?" Morrison demanded.

"I haven't the faintest idea."

"He was with you in the meadow. Didn't they bring him here?"

"No, certainly not."

Stella and Mrs. Cantor came pelting down the stairs, both swinging lanterns, to walk the few paces that took them from end to end of the room.

"She's killed and buried him. That's what it is," Mrs. Cantor decided. "See—see the tray up there with two cups and bowls on it."

"But one is from breakfast," I reminded her helpfully. "You didn't take the breakfast dishes away."

"You lying hussy! The wench is a witch!" she said to Stella, and backed a step away from me, lest I cast a spell on her.

"What have you done with the boy?" Stella demanded of Mrs. Cantor. "If you think you and Cantor are going to hide him and claim the reward for yourselves alone, think again. Wiggins will kill the pair of you. This is *our* operation. *We* found Beaudel, and *I* have lived with the old fool, sharing even my bed with him for six months. You'll not get away with this."

"He was *here,* I tell you. I saw him with my own eyes this very day. She's buried him in the coal. It's the only place he *could* be."

"Start shoveling then," Stella ordered. There was no shovel in the room, however.

"The poor woman must be insane," I said to Morrison, but in a loud enough voice for Stella to hear.

"Insane, is it?" Stella snorted. "A lying bitch is what she is." On this forthright speech, she gave the poor woman a hard clout across the head. The dame was too bewildered to reciprocate.

"He was *here,*" she insisted, but with a doubtful sound beginning to tinge her words now.

"I suppose this is some trick of yours," Stella said next, turning her wrath against Morrison.

"It is no trick," he answered reasonably. "Let us be sensible, think for a minute. Cantor and his wife snatched him from the garden. You haven't seen any of them since. Clearly, Cantor has taken the boy somewhere else. He must have asked his wife to lie for him, in case you came to check up. What we have to find out is where Cantor is." He turned to Mrs. Cantor. "Where is he?"

"He just went into town for a drink at the tavern. Don't worry he'll get drunk, Stella. You know he is as close as a jug. He won't say a word."

"*Idiot!* I told you both to stay here, not to take a step beyond the house. You bungled up the last job, letting Kersey's brat escape, and now you've bungled this one. If Cantor is running off at the mouth in a public tavern..."

"We'll go and find him," Morrison said. With a hand on my arm, he turned towards the stairs.

"Not *her*," Stella said, in the accents of a commander. "Not till I get the diamond, Major."

"I don't have it with me."

"You had it in your pocket when we left the Park. Give it to me if you expect to walk out of here with the girl."

"In that case, it looks like we leave the girl behind," he answered, with total indifference.

Stella looked at him, her brow furrowed with scheming. "What are you up to, Major? Why did you bother coming here if...? You never intended to give me the diamond at all. The girl was just an excuse to discover where Lucien was." There was suddenly a small pistol in her hand. I think she whipped it out of a skirt pocket, although it might have been hidden in her fingers all the time. "You've outsmarted yourself," she continued, glaring at Morrison.

"No, no. The diamond is in my carriage."

"I'll have a look for myself," she informed him, backing toward the stairs, the pistol leveled at him, whom she considered the most dangerous of her adversaries. Thus protected, she began backing up the stairs, carefully, one at a time.

"You'll never find it, love. Better let me go with you," he said, coaxingly.

"If it's there, I'll find it," was her reply. "And if it isn't, I'll come back and put a bullet through your head, and search your pockets. I know you had it when we left home. You'll be left here to rot with the rest of the garbage."

She reached the top step, flung back the door, and spun around into Mr. Mullins's waiting arms.

"I'll just take the weapon, miss," he said calmly, as he lifted it from her fingers.

"You took your sweet time getting here," Morrison grumbled, walking toward the stairs, pulling me behind him by the hand.

"Holy Faith and the Angels!" Mullins exclaimed. "What pickaninny is this you've found in the coal hole?"

"I have some hope it is Miss van Deusen, hiding under the dust," he answered, taking Mrs. Cantor by the arm to urge her up ahead of us. "Are you all right, Anna?" he asked, turning to gaze at me when we reached the top.

Stella was raising a noisy clamor, Mrs. Cantor countering with accusations and exclamations of her own; but I was hardly aware of it. I only knew the look Major Morrison turned on me was not the look of a murderer, or a vile person. There was worry, concern and love in his look. Also some shocked amusement at my condition.

"I don't know what could have happened to Lucien!" I said, and burst into tears of relief. He put his arms around me and made comforting sounds, as I destroyed his jacket with coal dust and tears, that were perfectly *black*.

There were other police than Mullins present. He had called in some reinforcements, probably local constables, who were full of self-importance to have real criminals to contend with, and only sorry they were women, who could not be treated as roughly as they would have liked.

"Someone is watching Wiggins?" Morrison asked over my shoulder.

"He's locked in a closet back at the Park, with a footman on guard outside with a pistol, dying for a chance to use it," Mullins told him. "He might be at the roundhouse by now."

"Send someone down to the pubs in Withamo to look for Cantor. He's the one who has Lucien," Morrison explained.

I had to correct this impression. Scant attention was paid to my babbling at first, but after Mullins had been to the cellar to see for himself the hole in the wall, he "deduced" I might be telling the truth. Between Morrison and Mullins, I had such a barrage of questions fired in rapid succession that I became incoherent, but at least they learned when he had left, in what direction he had been headed, and what his instructions had been.

"I have to go after him at once," Morrison told me. "One

of the men will take you back to the Park. You'll be safe there. You weren't hurt, other than the unfortunate surroundings below?"

"Not bludgeoned or anything like that."

"Good. I don't know how long we'll be, but from your appearance, a few days soaking in a tub will do you the world of good. I'll go to you as soon as possible."

"Yes. Be careful—Bertie?" I asked, with an excusable question in my voice, but the major did not notice any doubt in my choice of name for him.

He patted my cheek, with a half-distracted worried sort of a smile, then lifted my fingers to his lips. When they came away, coal dust decorated his own fingers, and probably his beard too, though its color hid it.

A constable, not Mullins, drove me back to Glanbury Park, via such a circuitous route, over bumpy lanes and narrow roads, that I had no more idea where I had been than before being rescued. I did know it was not the cottage hired in the name of Mr. Kirby though. The constable mentioned a village called Withamo as being the nearest settled area.

Chapter Eighteen

Even before I had time to wash my face or brush my hair, Mr. Beaudel asked me into his office. He had been hanging about the front door, wild with worry and apprehension for Lucien.

"It is true then," he said, sighing, when I told him my story. His first spate of questions was for Lucien's safety, but the dispirited sigh, I believed, was for his wife's complicity in the plot, for the final conviction that he had been a foolish old man, duped by a cunning, criminal woman. "I feared it must be so when they came and took away Wiggins. They were always so close, my wife and Wiggins."

Of course I did not tell him just how close they were, but he knew it. "You think the boy came to harm?" he queried next.

"He has been gone a very long time," I admitted. "But that is not to say he came to grief. He might be only lost."

"He is sensible for his age. I shan't give up hope till we

know for sure. His uncle, the fellow calling himself Morrison, seems very capable, though I don't see why he set about things in such an irregular manner."

"Morrison is Lord Sheldon, is he?"

"Yes, the youngest son of Sacheverel, but in the family they call him Bertie. It seems his father wrote off to him in India that he was displeased with my marriage—even *before* Algernon came home at Christmas and had a little falling out with Stella. Lord Sheldon was set to come home in any case, as he had made his fortune with the E.I.C. He stopped off to see Algernon at Cambridge, and had his ears filled with foolish stories. That is—stories," he amended sadly. "It was none of their business if I bought my wife pretty things, but Algernon took the idea I was spending his or his brother's money to do it. I was *not*. I *did borrow* five thousand pounds from Lucien to be sure, but wrote him an IOU and put it into a safe deposit box at the bank, so that he would be repaid if I should die before I could do it. And I planned to pay him interest on the loan till I could repay it too. My plan, you see, was to sell my own little property and hire a set of rooms in London for Stella and myself, after Algernon came home."

"Yes, you would not have been happy here, after Algernon returned," I said, feeling sorry for the old man.

"It was a very irregular way Lord Sheldon and Sacheverel set about the business," he repeated, shaking his head. "But they feared I was in league with Stella, you see, and that is why they mistrusted me a little. I was happy, that is, I *agreed* to lend them every assistance after I learned the whole truth. I even agreed to let Lord Sheldon borrow the rose diamond. I hope I did the right thing. He required it for something or other."

"You must have been relieved to learn it *was* the genuine Jaipur all the time."

"It is a great weight off my mind, I can tell you. What a fright to give an old man, and for no reason. I will be very happy to turn the running of the boys' affairs over to Sacheverel and his son. It has been nothing but a worry to me from the first. Soon Algernon will be back, and he will assume guardianship of his brother then. Lord Sheldon questioned why I decided to sell the collection, as Algernon will soon be here to handle matters, but I felt it for the best. Stella told me a dozen times I should do it, to let the interest pile up for Lucien you know, and I feared young Algernon would not have the wits to do it. He is young yet. I was only doing what I thought I ought."

"I really should go and clean up," I mentioned, with a glance at my filthy clothes.

"Of course. Go ahead, but I would appreciate talking to you again when you are ready. I shall be here, waiting," he said, with a weary, troubled sigh.

"I'll hurry," I told him.

Even with the utmost hurry, and utmost help from Tess and Cook in carrying kettles of hot water to my room, the removal of all the grime took an hour. My hair had to be washed and toweled dry. Most of all, I wanted food and drink. Cook sent up a roasted chicken and bread and tea, which I made a meal of while Tess dried my hair. Between bites, she heard the story.

"It don't surprise *me* one whit, and that's a fact," she said. "Only fancy that devil of a Lucien wriggling his way out a hole in the wall. Game as a fighting cock, the rascal. He'll get home safe and sound, miss, don't you worry your head."

"I expect he has got lost, wandering around, trying to find his way home."

"It don't seem like him, to be so slow about it. Why wouldn't he just *ask* someone? Anyone would be happy to bring a little lost boy home."

I disliked this line of thought, and tried to explain it away, but the fact was, he had been gone since sunrise, and it was now late at night. At least Stella and Wiggins did not have him.

When I returned to Beaudel's office, he sat with his head in his hands, looking as though he would groan with grief. I let him talk, to give relief to his remorse. For perhaps twenty minutes, I listened to him ramble on, explaining and excusing and exculpating his actions. "If anything happens to him..." he began, and stopped, unable to go on for the emotion that overwhelmed him.

We both jumped up when there was a banging at the front

183

door. "What can it be?" he exclaimed, becoming even paler, his eyes wilder.

"I'll see who it is," I said, as he sank back on to his chair, trembling.

One of the footmen had temporarily replaced Wiggins, and was at the door before me. The apparition that greeted my eyes was not one customarily seen at the *front* door of a respectable house, but at the servants' entrance. It was a bedraggled workman in a fustian coat, accompanied by what looked like a chimney sweep.

"You didn't have to knock, Mr. Fitz. I *live* here," the sweep said, in the unmistakable accents of Lucien Beaudel. A closer examination showed that beneath the sooty face and suit, perfectly covered with dirt, stood Lucien.

"Where have you *been*?" I shouted, grabbing him into my arms, to undo the work of an hour in cleaning myself.

"I've been taking care of the lad for you, at my place at Withamo," the man said, with an ingratiating tug at his forelock.

"I have been working with Mr. Fitz," Lucien replied matter-of-factly. "I *told* him I am not a 'prentice sweep, but he didn't believe me. In fact, he *lied* to the parish officer."

"Not exactly what you'd call a *lie!*" the man interjected swiftly.

"You said I was your 'prentice who had run away, and you know I'm not. But if I was, I *would*," he added, with an accusing look at his latest kidnapper.

"Didn't I save you from prison?" the man countered, with a baleful glare. "Arrested for stealing a loaf at the back door of the bakery, he was," he went on, nodding his head emphatically.

"Uncle Charles would have paid. It was for you, Miss Stacey," he added self-righteously.

"Ho, for the *lady,* was it, and yourself wolfing it down thirteen to the dozen. They took the wee tyke for a sweep, seeing as he was black from head to toe. So they called me, took me away from a big job at the manse, they did. To save the poor tyke from prison, miss, I allowed as he was one of my lads as had slipped the leash, as they will do from time to time, the beggars."

"I didn't say he was lying, so I would get out of prison faster," Lucien added. "But as soon as I got out, I *told* Mr. Fitz I had to go, and he wouldn't let me."

"Who'd believe such wild tales of kidnapping and locking up, and the little fellow looking no better off than a parish boy?" Mr. Fitz pointed out.

"He said if I tried to run off, he'd set his dogs on me. His dogs *eat* boys," he said, his eyes big as saucers. "I expect they are very hungry."

"Heh, heh, just keeping the laddie safe," the man said, with an ingratiating smile, made ludicrous by the lack of three-quarters of his teeth. "I daresay the man of the house will want to repay me for taking such good care of the lad," he added, lifting his head to glance beyond, into the house.

"I expect he will want to *see* you at least," I replied haughtily.

"As soon as ever the lad was ready for bed, and wanted to be taking off his clothes, and speaking of a *bath* and all, I knew he was real quality," the man said simply. Such extravagances were obviously not practiced in his circle.

"I cleaned four chimneys, Miss Stacey," Lucien boasted, not totally displeased. "And I am very hungry."

"He's had a *large* meal, miss."

"I told you I don't like pig's cheek," Lucien retaliated.

"You ate a good half of it!"

"It was a very small cheek."

"Chimney sweeps got to stay small, or they ain't fit for their work. They get stuck up the chimney. How would you like that, eh?"

"Please come this way," I said, with a sad thought for chimney sweeps in general.

Beaudel was already coming into the hallway. His delight in seeing Lucien safe was so great he did not question or harangue the man who had returned him, but gave him a generous pourboire, that displayed the man's few pegs of teeth in a broad smile.

"That's right handsome of you, sir. I took good care of your lad. Any time you want your chimneys swept out..."

"Leave your name and address with the servant," Beaudel said, and turned again to Lucien, to be assured he was unharmed. "Well, well, so you have turned chimney sweep, Lucien," he said, with the first smile of the evening.

"Yes, and I am very hungry, uncle."

"I'll put him in a tub first," I offered.

"That will be best," Beaudel agreed, handing him over to me.

"How did *you* get rescued, Miss Stacey?" Lucien asked, as we went upstairs, dropping a trail of cinders behind us.

"Major Morrison rescued me," I told him proudly.

"I knew he would. He is a great gun, ain't he?"

"He certainly is."

The boy was so fatigued from his unusual day that his lids were falling even while he manfully tried to eat his meal. "I'll finish this tomorrow," he said, yawning. "Just leave it here. I am still hungry," were his last words, as his head sank to the pillow. I removed the fork from his fingers gently, so as not to rouse him.

There was no way to let Morrison and the others know Lucien had returned. Until they checked back at the Park, we could do nothing but wait. During further conversations with Beaudel, I learned that Morrison had told him my true identity, and why I had come.

"I am convinced now your father never took the diamonds. It was a cruel stunt to play on him. Naturally the charge will be dropped. You don't suppose he will institute a counter-charge against me?" he asked fearfully.

"I'm sure he won't," I told him. No one could be cruel enough to further harass this unfortunate soul.

"I shall reimburse him handsomely for the time spent so uncomfortably in a cell."

"A man's reputation can't be paid for with money. What is important to him is that his name is cleared of any suspicion. A dealer in gems is only as good as his name," I pointed out.

"I didn't think of all that. What a deal of harm I have caused, by my blindness."

He had indeed caused inestimable mischief, not least to himself.

"They may not be back for hours. Why don't you go to bed, Mr. Beaudel? You look very tired."

"I am. I certainly am, but I doubt I'll sleep," he answered. As he went up the stairs, his stooped shoulders and lagging gait gave every appearance of advanced age. The rest of us involved would soon forget our unpleasant experience. I thought Beaudel would carry his memories to the grave.

Neither the servants nor I had any intention of going to bed before the others returned. They were eager to hear all the details, and I was eager to see Lord Sheldon. It was well after midnight before they returned, disheartened by a lack of success.

"You mean he's been here all the time!" Morrison howled. I could not think of him as anyone but Major Morrison. Not yet. It would be perfectly feasible for a major to marry a gem merchant's daughter. I was coming to think a younger son of a lord, providing he had his own fortune, might also find it feasible, and wished I had time to call in a coiffeur and buy powder for my nose.

"Only for a few hours," I said, and brought them up to date.

"We've got the woman and Wiggins and their two helpers in custody," Constable Harper said. "Tomorrow will be time enough to lay formal charges. We'll need your help, my lord, and yours, Miss van Deusen."

"Could my father not be let out of prison now?" I asked.

"He'll be sound asleep, Anna," Morrison pointed out. "We'll do it first thing in the morning. Best not to disturb him, don't you think?"

"You're right of course. It is very late."

It was not too late for Cook to regale them all with coffee and cold meat, and to listen while the story was fully explained. Not all parts of it were told to the outsiders. Not until I was alone with Bertie did certain points come to light.

"Beaudel told me why you came, but why did you decide to come as Major Morrison?" I asked.

"It was Algernon's idea really. I grew the beard on the ship coming home from India. Every man wants to grow a beard once in his life, and that seemed the perfect time. I stopped at Cambridge to see my nephew, and hear firsthand what was afoot here that had worried him enough to write to my father. He was trying to have Stella and Wiggins in-

187

vestigated by a man he hired, but the fellow dragged his heels, and didn't really learn much. If I had come as myself, I might have been shown the door. Beaudel is the legal guardian, not accountable to me, or even to my father. My Indian skin needed some excuse, so I hit on the obvious one—the Peninsula, which also allowed me to keep my whiskers, just in case Beaudel saw some resemblance to my sister in me. Beaudel knew her quite well, you know. We feared Lucien might not keep the secret if we told him, so Algernon gave me his ring. He had spoken to Lucien at Christmas, having some intention then of putting a spy into the house, which he didn't do after all. He hired Miss Little though, and was in close touch with her. She'll be returning, after this little vacation I arranged."

"But you didn't come as Major Morrison originally. You were Mr. Kirby first."

"I stopped at London after seeing Algernon. My intention was to have an expert examine the collection, to see if it was intact. Algernon knew Stella was after Charles to sell it, and thought he might be open to a bid. That much I learned from my father's first letter. As soon as she married Charles, she started this idea of selling. It was that as much as anything that set Sacheverel against the woman. He is all in favor of keeping it in the family. I don't know that it will be possible. Lucien *will* require some monies, as he matures, but he certainly does not need a hundred thousand pounds at his age."

"What trouble did you expect? You mentioned it in the letter to Papa."

"Pieces missing, forgeries, substitutions. I don't know. I gave Dutch a list of the important pieces, and a description. I certainly didn't expect they'd try to pin the crime on *him*! Once that happened, Mr. Kirby rapidly became Major Morrison, dashing to the rescue."

"And making Mr. Kirby unavailable when we needed him."

"I meant to tell you sooner."

"Why didn't you?"

"You won't like my reason," he cautioned, with a wary look. "Pray remember I had never met your father. I had just got back from a long stint in India, and chose him on the word of an acquaintance, who did not know him personally. He did not say he was *honest*. There was a chance he *had* stolen the diamonds, and likewise a possibility he had sent you down here to help him in some manner."

"You thought we were thieves!"

"Subsequent inquiries assured me it was not the case. All right, you won't like the other reason any better, but here it is. I thought if you knew I could get your father out of jail quickly, you would pester me to do it. You have such a winning way, Anna. It suited me better to let Stella and Wiggins think their schemes were not suspected. Dutch agreed to sit tight while I laid my snares to entrap them."

"It was foolish of us not to think they would kidnap *Lucien.*"

"Stella was to be the victim, originally. It was only when Beaudel began to think she had snaffled the Jaipur, and looked at her with a less loving eye, that she feared he wouldn't pay up for her. I believe the Cantors were notified the night you went to Kirby's cottage. Wiggins was also out, remember?"

"Yes, Tess thought I was with him."

"You may imagine how I felt when I learned my mistake. The deuce of it was we never learned where the cottage was, that they had hired to hold Lucien. We always assumed we'd grab them before they had occasion to use it. We didn't even know you and Lucien were gone for a couple of hours. Mullins and I were on the *qui vive* at the house, watching Stella and Wiggins, who went about their normal activities like a couple of professional actors. When we finally realized it was time you and Lucien were coming back and went after you, we wasted another hour searching orchards and stables and I don't know what all. God, what a nightmare, as it slowly sank in what had happened. And after *I* sent you out there too."

"As a matter of fact, Stella made a point of checking to see I was taking him out that afternoon."

"Was it very bad?" he asked sympathetically.

"You saw the accommodations. You didn't have to taste the food." The worst of it, I did not mention—that I thought *he* was a thieving impostor.

189

"I was so happy to see you alive, I didn't take much notice of the accommodations. It was impossible not to notice you had changed color, of course."

"What I have been wondering is how you ever talked Stella into leading you to me."

"It wasn't easy. I can't remember when I have told so many lies as I have the past week. It went more or less like this. To convince Beaudel his wife was behind the kidnapping, I had to take him completely into my confidence—my real identity, Algernon's suspicions, the report from Tunbridge Wells, the lot. He already knew she didn't care a tinker's curse for him—he *knew* it, but tried to pretend he didn't, to himself even, I mean. The ransom demand came in the mail the morning after you two were taken away. Charles let on he was going to pay up, but once we got a look at the details, we saw there was no way of trapping them during the exchange of money for boy. He was to take a case full of cash to London, along a predetermined route, on the mail coach. Alone, of course. There were dozens of chances of a foulup, but most of all was the time involved. None of us could endure a week's delay. The thirty or so hours you were gone seemed an eternity. Worrying, remorse—God, I feel as old as Beaudel looks."

"We never would have lasted a week without going insane."

"Neither would we. So I went to Stella and made her another offer. I told her I was a con man, like herself, come to steal the Jaipur. She already thought a fake was in the safe, so she wasn't hard to convince I had the original. Beaudel loaned it to me. I showed it to her, and told her it was hers if she'd take me to you."

"She must have thought you were very fond of me!"

"I am, but she wouldn't understand love. She really doesn't even love Wiggins, but only finds him a useful tool. I told her you were my accomplice, and I had to get you back. We—ah—discussed disposing of you terminally, but I convinced her that besides my having some designs on your body, you were negotiating to become governess for the Duchess of Devontree. The Dowager Duchess, you know, has a very fine collection of jewelry. My story was probably shot full of holes,

190

if she had sat down and thought about it, but I kept flashing the diamond at her, and tempting her greed, and rushing her like the devil. I told her I had to leave that night, with or without you, but preferably with. In the end, she agreed to slip out of the house with me after dark, and take me to you. The name of Lucien was not even mentioned in my priorities. I am by no means sure either of us would have been allowed to leave alive. Your little surprise in having lost Lucien upset the girl. That was very clever, letting on he had never been there. How'd you come to think of it?"

"I learned the trick of setting thieves at each other's throats from you, Bertie."

"Thank you. Here Mullins has been telling me *he* takes the credit, as he gave you some lessons in logic."

"It was inspiration, not logic."

"Whatever it was, it worked. Stella cropped out into a nice, incriminating confession before two witnesses—you and me. She would have had more in a minute. The police were to storm in five minutes behind me, or sooner, if they heard shots or other ominous sounds."

"You arrranged to have them follow you and Stella?"

"I'd never have found you, if she hadn't taken me to you. It was only desperation that pushed me to offer her the diamond. Greed is a terrible thing. It blinds folks to reason."

"Love is as bad. Poor Beaudel—what a monkey she made of him."

"At his age too. He ought to know better. It is excusable in young whippersnappers like ourselves. I hope you aren't rehearsing to renounce me on the grounds that love is bad for the use of reason," he said, as he grabbed me into his arms, raking my cheek with his beard.

"I wouldn't dream of it, Bertie. I have much better grounds for renouncing you. Lying, impersonating an officer——" He covered my lips with his and kissed me, tickling my chin with his beard, so that I laughed and spoiled it. "Getting my father tossed into jail, and me..."

"And *you* a very eligible husband. Don't forget *that* in your list of crimes! Dutch let it slip how *desperate* he is, to find you a presentable parti." After a heavy frown, he kissed me again, more forcefully, so that I forgot the beard, and all the wretched consequences of his interference in our lives. It had been worth it after all.

The early part of the morning Bertie and Beaudel spent at the courts, signing complaints and testimony against the infamous Stella and Wiggins. By eleven, my father was at last out of jail, and before noon, he came to Glanbury Park with the other men, for his final view of the Jaipur. He was wreathed in smiles, and delighted to be rid of me. He was also full of potential customers for the Jaipur.

"I'll tell you who would pay top pound for it—the old Dowager Duchess of Devontree. She covets unique gems of this sort. I usually get a five-percent commission for arranging mutually satisfactory bargains of this sort," he added.

"No, no, we are in no hurry to sell," Bertie told him, while Beaudel hemmed and hawed, afraid to open his mouth, for fear of displeasing someone.

It was several weeks before the matter was finalized. With such reluctance to sell, it was necessary for the Dowager to go as high as 65,000 guineas, and Papa as low as two percent on his fee. It was sufficient to give his daughter a decent wedding, as she modestly declined any dowry. What Bertie calls his "chicken stake," and the rest of us call his fortune, is more than sufficient to keep us in style in London. Neither of us has any desire to remove to the country, which displeases Sacheverel nearly as much as the sale of the Jaipur. He will be even more displeased to hear his son is turning tea merchant, so we will be at pains to see he does not hear it.

I like my husband much better without his whiskers, and decline every offer on his part to grow them again. They remind me too sharply of my ordeal at Glanbury Park. Sir Algernon is installed there now, taking care of Lucien, and chasing after all the local girls. He bought back all of Lucien's collection that Bertie purchased, thank goodness. Lucien, who writes to me occasionally, suspects Miss Little has set her cap at Algernon, and is giving her every assistance in her quest. She could not have a better go-between, in my opinion. Lord Sheldon urges the suit on his nephew. He claims he is very satisfied that the governesses from Glanbury Park make excellent wives.

192